BENNETT. THE HAWK ALONE.

Gord Vance, aging South African hunter,
finds himself at odds with the new age and
its reckless destruction of wild life and
wilderness. The story reaches its tragic
climax when he leads a safari for a group of
hard drinking, callous and contemptuous teen-
agers.

The Hawk Alone

JACK BENNETT

The Hawk
Alone

Boston · Toronto

LITTLE, BROWN AND COMPANY

The Hawk Alone

1

The big lioness had taken two heavy bullets, fired from too far and without thought, and now she had stopped running and lay in the long yellow grass.

Gord looked at the grass, swaying gently in the soft wind, and watched the young American moving nearer on his very good horse that probably already had the tsetse-fly poison in its thoroughbred blood, and thought: I wish they would let me do this my way.

But they were rich Americans and they were townspeople and above all they were paying, and they wanted to do it their way. Gord watched the moving grass and tried to imagine the lioness lying there, thirsty and in pain, her mouth frothed with red saliva, carrying two .375 bullets in her golden body, but his mind shied away from the picture.

He watched the man and the nervous horse go nearer. The rest of the party was spread out in a crescent fifty yards from the grass, the five Chagga beaters and old Mr. Jones, the young man's father. Gord lifted his rifle and settled it into the hollow of his shoulder. He had no faith in the young man on the horse.

Mr. Jones walked across to Gord, his boots noisy on the hard earth. Gord kept his eyes on the grass.

"What do you think, Gord?" Mr. Jones was apologetic.

"Should've let me go after her," said Gord, watching the moving grass.

"Think she's hit badly?" asked Mr. Jones. They had heard the two bullets smack into her as she ran, belly low, for the bush.

"It was too far," said Gord. "And the angle was wrong. You should've let her go."

"I was excited," said Mr. Jones. "I got carried away. And I never thought I'd hit her."

"You did, didn't you?" said Gord.

"It was just a snap shot," said Mr. Jones. He sounded hurt. He had thought it was pretty good shooting. He had white hair and his face was very pink with new sunburn and he had rimless dark glasses and a hat with a cheetah-skin band.

"Buck's all right," said Mr. Jones, watching his son and the horse moving along near the edge of the grass. "He can shoot okay, Gord. That youngster can shoot."

"I've seen him," said Gord. "I know he can shoot. But this is different."

He watched Buck put his horse nearer the grass. Buck was sitting very relaxed, his rifle lying across the saddle in front of him. He was a very big young man on a very big horse and he was quite sure of himself.

"She's dead, probably," said Mr. Jones hopefully, watching the grass. "Do you think so?"

"No." said Gord. "You didn't hit her anywhere bad. She

was too far away and the angle was wrong. I told you not
to shoot unless you got a good shot."

Mr. Jones looked away. He was beginning to find Gord
a bore.

Gord turned and looked at the spaced line of men. The
beaters were frightened. They were ready to run. He could
see that by the way they walked. The lioness had been
wounded by bad shooting in bad light just after sunrise
and they wanted to keep away from her.

The wind was blowing from the west, very softly, and
some dew still sparkled on the overnight spider webs. On
the horizon there was a line of low clouds. It was a good
day. Gord wished it were all over so they could enjoy the
day together, if that was possible.

Buck was on the edge of the grass. He shouted, standing
in the stirrups, slapping the horse's rump with his big hat.
The horse shied nervously. He got a whiff of her then,
thought Gord. He got a whiff of her then, all right.

Buck dropped the reins and lifted his Mannlicher and
fired a round into the grass. The horse shied again and then
Gord saw the grass quiver as the lioness came out, coming
through the grass in a low run, silently, with the big male
behind her growling in a long low gargle.

"Jesus," said Mr. Jones.

Buck fired once, high and hopelessly, and put his heels
into the mare. Gord saw her drop her hindquarters and
bunch, and then she froze as the lioness cleared the grass.
Buck shouted once as the lioness came over the mare's rump
and pulled him out of the saddle.

[5]

"*Jesus!*" *screamed Mr. Jones.* "*Shoot, shoot, please for God's sake shoot!*"

He got his heavy express up to his shoulder and the first shot hit the mare. She screamed and fell, kicking, and Gord could see the lioness lying over Buck. His whole head seemed to be in her mouth. Mr. Jones fired again, sobbing, and the bullet went off into the bush.

Gord gave her two, very quickly, behind the shoulder, and she fell forward, stretching her legs out behind her very slowly, like a cat lying in the sun.

The mare was still kicking. Gord turned and looked for the lion. Mr. Jones was behind him. He had broken the express and jammed a cartridge in the breech.

The beaters were running. The lion was hesitating, undecided, when he saw Gord. He dropped low, grunting, and then came on in a rush, tail low and straight behind him. Gord kept the .303 on him until he was twenty yards away and then shot him just below the start of the mane.

They got Buck out from under the lioness and put a tourniquet on the remains of his arm. He was conscious and very shocked. The earth around him was dark red and muddy with blood. His jaw was broken and this gave his face a strange laughing look. The lioness had bitten him across the face and when Gord cleared some of the blood away Mr. Jones started crying.

The beaters came back and they made a stretcher and put Buck on it. He was unconscious now and breathing very badly. While they were doing all this the wounded mare lay watching them, her breath raising little puffs of dust. Mr. Jones's bullet had hit her in the stomach. Gord shot her

[6]

*from behind and reloaded the Lee-Enfield and they started
to carry Buck home.*

*"You know why they call him Buck?" asked Mr. Jones,
after a mile.*

*"No," said Gord. He did not want to know. He had had
enough of them.*

*"Because he's like him. The cowboy, you know. The
Hollywood star. Ready for anything. He wanted to lasso
a rhino up in Uganda last year, you know, had his rope and
everything, but he never got the chance. Then we decided
to come down here."*

There were flies and dust on the boy's face.

*"He's just a cowboy." said Mr. Jones. "Mr. Buck Jones."
He glanced at the boy with his bloody dusty face and
started crying again.*

*It was fifty miles to Nairobi. Buck Jones never made ten
of them.*

2

THE wind was blowing from the ocean, a long way away. Before it reached the house on the red clay hill it had blown over miles of hot plain, tumbleweed, tortured thorn. It was like the gritty breath of a fever patient. You would never have thought it had started on the cool water.

It blew around the wood-frame house with strange buffetings, rising and falling. All the time Gord could hear the steady soft sifting of sand against the corrugated iron outer walls, the slight flexing and creaking of the roof sheets, the insidious whisper of fine sand coming in under the eaves and spreading down over the house like a fine mist. When the lulls came he could hear the sudden wild chatter of a hammer drill in the road gang down at the drift. They were tarring the main road through to the north. At first the engineers had fascinated him. He had spent hours watching them, watching the bulldozers tear huge gobs of earth out of the hillside, the big graders shuttling back and forth like monstrous animals. Then he had walked back up the hills outside the town and seen the black ribbon of the new tar road stretching straight as a ruled line across the drab

[8]

yellow-green bush, a shining black line puddled with gleaming water mirages, and he had become suddenly afraid. Now he no longer watched the work, but each day the clatter of the drill and the roaring and clanking of the bulldozers grew nearer, creeping up the dirt road towards the house.

This windy autumn morning Gord came out of the house and stood for a while on the stoep, his eyes screwed up against the flying dust. Down in the valley the roofs of the little town shimmered in the heat haze. A long way behind the town the worn red hills reared up into tumbled blue mountains. Although it was autumn the hot dry weather had held. There was still no new green in the bush. The leaves of the dusty low hedge below the stoep frittered drily, like cut paper. Gord walked slowly down the worn stone steps and the wind beat about him. He went across the dead and dry garden, the crusts of red clay crunching beneath his feet, and swung open the doors of the lean-to garage. He hooked the doors back carefully and went into the hot dark shed with its smell of bat droppings, and old engine oil and paraffin. His old saddle and bridle were slung over a beam. He walked around the humpbacked Ford and touched the good leather softly. It was a Western-style saddle with a very high pommel. He stood there in the dark, listening to the wind slamming around the shed, feeling and smelling the well-tended leather, and he felt suddenly good for the first time in weeks. It was an old saddle and a very good one in its day and he had looked after it very well. He had not used it for nearly a year, but he still took it down once a week and examined it for signs of damp or wear. Up

[9]

until the end of the last shooting season he had kept his own horse, a gaunt chestnut called Comet, but that year the horse had turned sixteen and become nearly blind, so that it blundered into bushes, and its joints had suddenly stiffened so that when it lay down it could only get up painfully, in huge jerks and creakings. With the first frost Comet had seized up completely, standing scruffy and unresponsive in the crackling yellow grass, unable even to bend his neck to feed. He had stood in the same spot all morning, and at midday, when his tired old joints had thawed, he had followed Gord around as he worked in the garden, nudging his muzzle into the man's back nervously every few minutes, as though frightened of being left alone. That evening he slowed down again and after supper Gord saw him standing forlornly under the old fir tree near the crossroads, his head hanging down, a hind leg pulled up uncomfortably. Gord took down the Mauser and walked the old horse around to the deep municipal rubbish tip behind the house, and, standing him right on the brink, shot him between the eyes. He was sorry about the horse. He had been very fond of it. But more than that: the horse had been another link with his past, and now it was dead. He knew then that he would never go back. He was sixty-nine that year and he had recently started wearing glasses but he reckoned he could still shoot as well as anyone in the country. He had always been a good snapshot, even using an Army model Lee-Enfield with a peep-sight.

He turned away from the saddle and opened the door of the old Ford and slid behind the wheel. He pulled out the choke and when he pulled the starter the big engine churned over a few times and then fired hesitantly. He sat there in the dim shed for five minutes, with the blue exhaust smoke swirling across the shafts of sunlight, until the V–8 settled down into a steady rhythm. There was a slight knock developing which worried him. It sounded like a main bearing. He was not worried about his mechanical ability. He knew he could fix it all right, if he borrowed a block and tackle to haul the engine out with, and paid a kaffir a few bob to help with the heavy work. But if it was a main you usually found half a dozen other things needed doing. He sighed unhappily and sat listening to the traitorous tick-tick in the engine. It was audible even above the slapping of loose pistons and the rattle of worn valves. He felt a slow deep resentment at his dependence on this mechanical thing. He backed the car out of the shed and drove up to the house. He had never liked cars.

"You going into town, Gord?" said his wife. She poured tea in the small kitchen, helping him to milk and sugar, a strong, stocky woman of fifty with gray hair parted in the middle and caught up in two small braids behind her ears. Her complexion was deep brown, the color of oiled wood, and very good for her age, smooth and shining. She came from a very religious family and had never used makeup. She had stayed single until she met and married Gord Vance when she was thirty-nine. She watched him now as he drank his tea: very tall, straight still, thin as a ridgeback dog, his white hair cut very short so that his skull showed all brown and knobby through it. He had not shaved that morning and his cheeks and jaw were peppered with short white stubble. His eyes were deepset and very blue and

faded without having lost their brightness or their direct-
ness. He was wearing scuffed brown velskoens without
socks, almost white from much scrubbing, a short-sleeved
new khaki shirt, and old khaki trousers, frayed at the cuffs.
His skin was a very deep brown and on his arms the texture
was still good but on his face and neck the flesh had retreated so that there were folds and creases. He still held
himself very well and walked well. But she knew that he
now had to think about doing these things and that worried
her.

"I'm driving down," he said. "Do you want anything? I've
got to get some cartridges."

"I think I've got everything," she said, watching him. He
stood up, smoothing down his trousers.

She still could not believe her good fortune. She looked
at him now and wondered again what it would have been
like if they had had any children. Being childless had not
worried her. Gord had been the oasis in the desert of her
spinsterhood. Now she was resting by the water and had no
desire for any further trek. She would wake up sometimes
at night and feel him lying beside her and there in the dark
hot room tears of gratitude would well up and run down
her cheeks. She prayed every night and she always asked
God to let her die first. She reproached herself for being
selfish but she was terribly afraid of being alone again.

He kissed her and went out. She sat listening to him
cross the creaking hall and waited until she heard the car
grumble down the hill. She sat in the kitchen for a while
after the last sounds had died, hearing the wind beating the
house, the fine sifting of the sand, the far-off clatter of the

road gang. The clock ticked very loudly in the hall. She got up at last and heated water on the wood stove for the washing up.

Gord drove down the national road to the town. The road was raw gravel and ran along an exposed high ridge. The wind slammed into the car and lifted clouds of grit from the road. There were no trees beside the road to break the wind, just low scrub.

During the Boer War he had been with a transport column which had been caught on a ridge just like this, in the Orange Free State. (Only now it was bad form to talk about it as the Boer War. It was now officially the South African War and still, after forty-four years, capable of arousing more ill feeling in the country than either of the World Wars.) He remembered it now. He remembered it most days he rode this road. He remembered the panting sound of the shells in the cold air as they went over. They could not stop there so they whipped up the teams and went on, and the shells started dropping farther down the ridge. He remembered standing up in the stirrups and watching them explode with flat thuds down among the scrub; then the Krupps found the range and marched up the ridge and started falling among the train. The explosions could be felt more than heard: they slammed air against the ears so that men cried out. The shrapnel made a high sweet singing sound in the winter afternoon. As he drove into town now he realized that it was forty-four years ago.

3

THE town was built of gray-brown stone. The pepper trees along the streets were the same dull shade. Only the hibiscus hedge around the convent school had any color. The pavements were wide and the gutters were shallow and wide, always carrying a trickle of water from the reservoir on the hill behind the town. There was no water reticulation in the town. Each house had its own rainwater tank and septic tank, and water for the gardens was led off the gutters through channels controlled by small sluice gates. If you walked along the pavements and shut your eyes the constant cool trickling of the water in the wide gutters created the illusion that you were in a cool and green valley. Then you opened your eyes and the reality hurt: the small ugly town, the featureless dusty roads stirring in the hot wind, the listless drab trees, the bare red hills ringing the valley. In winter the wind blew down cold from the hills, laying a thin crust of ice over the puddles in the rutted streets. The hotels were like the town itself: small and mean and depressed. It was no pleasure to drink in them. The small palms in the grounds of the Royal Hotel jutted uncomfort-

ably on the balding lawn, their stringy fronds frittering
drily in the wind. The Royal Hotel was double-storied, with
a wide surrounding stoep of rough, red-polished cement,
sheltered by a curving roof of rust-patched corrugated iron.
Inside it was dark and narrow, the floors covered with
linoleum from which the pattern had long been eroded.
Gord drove into town, past the Royal Hotel and the tired
palms, and parked the Ford in the main street. The wind
was stronger now, whipping sand and scraps of paper along
the street. He walked across the road to Pithey's General
Dealer, Guns and Ammunition a Speciality, and went inside. The shop was dark and cool, smelling of leather, cordite, soap, bulk sugar, and cleaning oil. He stood just inside
the door for a moment, letting his eyes adjust to the dark,
smelling the old good smells. This shop reminded him of a
Chinaman's shop in his home town. That's strange, he
thought. I can remember that. I can remember fifty years
back, but I forget what happened last week. Last week is
like a hundred years ago, and half a life back is like last
week. Cordite and oil and paraffin and soap, sugar and flour
and cheap gaudy sweets and bright blankets piled on the
shelves, silent mud-faced Africans sitting in their blankets,
bright beads and chewing tobacco and coffee like dark
earth sold in cones of twisted paper . . . He walked to the
counter. Tom Pithey was showing a single-shot Remington
to a customer, a young farmer whom Gord did not know.

"Morning, Gord," Tom said. He was a short square man
with thick dark hair and a heavy jaw. He left the young
farmer and came across to Gord.

[15]

"I've been wanting to see you, Gord. Hoped you'd come in."

"Yes?" said Gord. He wished the young farmer were not in the shop.

"Tom," he said. He glanced at the young farmer, hoping Tom would move further down the counter.

"Yes?" said Tom. He stood where he was, his wide hands flat on the wooden counter top.

"I need some cartridges, Tom. Couple of boxes of buckshot, and a box of three-o-three."

"Oh," said Pithey. He looked away, nervously.

"I'd like to, Gord, You know I would. But your account's pretty high, Gord. You didn't give me anything last month."

"I thought, just this month," said Gord. "I need these cartridges. I mean I've got something come up, and I can't afford to be caught short."

"Hell, Gord, you know I trust you," said Pithey. "It's just that I can't extend you any more credit."

He glanced anxiously towards the back of the long shop, to where his wife sat at an old school desk. She ran the shop. She kept the books; did the stock buying, interviewing salesmen like an inquisitor (while Tom hovered in the background); granted credit when she thought the customer was reliable, which was very seldom, and tongue-lashing publicly any debtor who lapsed in his payments.

"Can't do it, Gord," said Pithey, lowering his voice. "You know I'd like to, but I just can't."

Gord put his hand in the breast pocket of his khaki shirt and took out his government pension check. Pithey watched him with careful eyes.

[16]

"You can cash this for me?" asked Gord. He endorsed the check with the counter's steel dip-pen and held it out. "Take two quid out of it?"

"You got something lined up?" asked Pithey. The young farmer had finished examining the rifle and was looking at them.

"Yes," said Gord.

Pithey shrugged and took the check. He pushed two cartons of shotgun shells and one of .303 ammunition across the counter to Gord. He put the check in the till and counted out some notes and silver.

"That's two quid off your account and one off this lot," he said. "Leaves seven." He counted the old notes out on to the wood and laid the silver on them. "All right?"

"Thank you," said Gord. He took the notes and put them in his top pocket. He wanted to go now.

"Hear you had a row with Doctor Hammersley," said Pithey.

"No row, no," said Gord.

"Hear you walked out on him and that young bloke from Grahamstown."

"No," said Gord. "They wanted a buck. I took them out and they each got a buck. Then I came home."

"That's not the way I heard it," said Pithey.

"That's the way it was," said Gord. He turned away. He just wanted to go now.

"Look Gord," said Pithey. "Look. You got to understand these people. They buy a big farm with plenty of game, they want to hunt it their way. It's their property. They paid for it. You be reasonable with Doctor Hammersley, you could probably do all the vermin shooting on his place. There's plenty baboons, jackals, dassies in those kloofs. Even leopard and rooikat. Could be a nice little income. He's going to shoot the place out, right? So why shouldn't you benefit?"

"The game laws still apply," said Gord. "Even on private property."

"I wouldn't try that," said Pithey. "I wouldn't try that, Gord. You just got to realize people don't worry about that stuff any more. Game in reserves, yes. On private farms, no. And it's reasonable. I ask you, isn't it reasonable?"

Gord picked up the cartridges.

"Don't worry, Tom," he said. "You'll get your money."

"Hell, Gord, you know that's not it. That's not it at all. Haven't I always carried you?"

"And let me know it," said Gord. He turned and walked out. Pithey followed him to the door.

"That's the way you feel," he said, "go somewhere else." He shut the door and walked back into the shop. The young farmer, who had found the conversation very entertaining, was examining the rifle again. He handed it back to Pithey.

"I'll think about it," he said.

"Sorry about that," said Pithey. "That old — "

"Yes," said the young man. "Well, I'll let you know."

He went out. Pithey sat down and wiped his face. He thought being a shopkeeper was extremely difficult. Nobody understood you. He opened the cash register and took out Gord's check. It was a brown government check. He must be pretty bad, thought Pithey, to be cashing his pension check for ammunition. Pretty bad. He sat there turning the check over in his fingers. "Hell, what can I do," he said aloud. "What the hell can I do? I don't look after myself now, I end up like that. Like hell. No thank you. What the hell." After a while another customer came in and Tom Pithey stopped feeling bad.

4

At that hour of the morning the air was still very cold and the ground was white with frost. They went down into the kloof, Gord walking ahead and the townsmen following him, their breath hanging on the frozen air. There was a low white mist curling around the bush in the bottom of the kloof. They found the dry watercourse and walked along it. Down towards the end of the kloof the bush thinned and they came out into a shallow valley of thin grass, anthills, and low thorn trees. They kept to the side of the valley, walking carefully and quietly among the tall scraggy euphorbia trees, watching the open country. A hundred yards away a flock of guinea fowl were feeding, running back and forth in their jerky way, like windup toys. The men could hear their soft t-t-t-t-rrr cries as they scrabbled for grass roots in the hard red earth. The townsman with the double-barrelled twelve-bore shotgun lifted the gun and looked along the barrel, nuzzling his cheek against the stock. Gord shook his head. They walked on slowly, stepping carefully on the dead vegetation beneath the trees. The guinea fowl scuttled into the trees with frightened cries. At the end of the euphorbias they stood and looked out over a narrow draw where the valley dropped away sharply to the river. It was cold and damp under the trees. The sun was just touching the top of the hills across the river. Gord guessed it must be about six o'clock. He wished it were over. He wished these townsmen had shot their buck and gone home. He wanted to get back to the homestead and have a cup of coffee and then drive back to his house just outside the town. The townsmen leaned against the tree boles and rubbed their hands and thighs. Gord fed a cartridge into the chamber of his service model Lee-Enfield .303 and put the safety on. He was wearing thick woollen gloves with the fingers cut out. He did not like wearing gloves at all but in the last year he had started feeling the cold very much. He stood with the rifle in both hands watching the thick bush along the river. Somewhere a pheasant called and up in the euphorbias he heard a monkey chitter warningly.

"Better be ready," he said quietly. The townsmen straightened up and stood beside him. The older one of the two had just bought this farm from a friend of Gord's. He was a retired doctor and he liked shooting. He had paid a good price for the farm because it had more game on it than any other farm in the district. Gord's friend had been a conservationist and a most selective hunter. The retired doctor had done a lot of hunting in South Africa and Rhodesia, but he was still a bad shot and a man who knew nothing at all about the bush and wanted to know nothing. All he asked of his guides was that they put the required animal before him. The younger man was a rising young

*lawyer who had driven up from Grahamstown for the week-
end. Both men had very good guns. The retired doctor had
a long double twelve-bore by Greener of London and the
younger man had a Winchester pump-action twelve. Gord
did not think much of men who used shotguns for buck.*

*The doctor broke his gun and the ejector slid two thick
green shells out into his hand.*

"I've got an SSG and a Number Six," he said. "That do?"

*"Put a Three-A in the choke. Six's too small for buck,"
said Gord.*

*"I've shot duiker with a ten," said the younger man. He
worked the slide and pumped a round into the chamber.*

*The doctor took out the Number Six and slid in another
round. Gord watched him. He wondered how many buck
the lawyer had wounded with small shot.*

*The bushbuck ram came out of the bush first, treading
warily, keeping close up to the thorn. They could see little
puffs of vapor from his nostrils. Gord watched him come
daintily down the slope and imagined the small sharp
hooves cutting crisply through the dew-firmed earth. The
ram had small black horns and his coat was a deep choc-
olate brown with white markings on the lower hindquarters
and a crest of coarser hair along his rump. Gord guessed
he was a young ram. The doctor raised his gun and then
the ewe and the fawn slipped out of the bush and came
down the slope to the ram. The ewe dislodged a stone and
shied nervously as it rattled down the path. The doctor's
gun moved upwards and followed the animals and Gord
shook his head and then his ears sang as the twelve-bore
fired. The ram skidded sideways and fell and rolled over*

kicking and got up and ran in a circle, turning back towards the men under the trees. The doctor fired again and the ram fell and stayed down, and then the ewe and the fawn, panicked and not knowing where the noise had come from, ran towards the shelter of the high euphorbias, and at ten yards the lawyer hit her just where the tail joins the body. At that range the heavy shot struck her like a steel fist and she went down trailing her shattered hindquarters, screaming and pawing at the hard earth with her forelegs. The lawyer pumped another round at her but the shot was not spreading and he missed, the pellets making a silver smear on the hard clay. Gord swore and shot her through the head as quickly as he could and jacked another round into the breech just in time to see the doctor, who had reloaded, shoot the fawn as it stood petrified with shock. The small body flopped over like a trick target in a sideshow as the shot slammed into it. Gord swung the Lee-Enfield up and around and the doctor stopped with his shotgun halfway open and smiled uncertainly. Gord lowered his rifle and the doctor ejected the empty cartridge case. The short expended shells from the shotguns lay smoking slightly in the thin grass and the cordite smell was strong on the still air. The three buck lay without moving. Ten feet up something dangled from a euphorbia tree and dripped steadily onto the leaves below: the ewe's stubby tail, blown off her by the explosive force of a charge of SSG at thirty feet.

They left the buck for the skinners and walked back to the pickup at the head of the kloof without speaking.

5

GORD walked slowly along the main street. He went
into the public bar of the Criterion Hotel and had a brandy
and water. The bar was empty at that hour. The barman
was an old man with stooped shoulders. Gord sat there for
an hour. He made the brandy last. It was a long time since
he had had a drink and he could taste every drop. When it
was finished he felt like another but he thought of his wife
sitting alone in the house on the hill, alone in the nearly
empty house, and he decided not to. He went out and
picked up some groceries and put three gallons of low-grade
in the Ford and drove slowly home. I should sell her, he
thought, listening to the tick-tick in the engine. I really
should sell her. If I still had a horse I'd sell her. But if I
sell her I have nothing at all. He imagined them trapped
in the house on the hill forever, marooned by the immobility
of old age.

On the crest of the hill he stopped the car and sat watching the road gang. The noise, and the clouds of dust across
the bush. He started the Ford and drove down to the detour
which diverted traffic around the new highway. This close

the clatter of the jackhammers and the bellowing diesels
was a thundering tumult of sound. He sat and watched the
bulldozers bite into the red earth. They were open-seat bulldozers; the drivers were dressed in high boots, overalls, and
gauntlets, with cloths wrapped around their heads to keep
the dust out of their hair. The dust lay so thickly on them
that Gord could not see whether they were Africans or
Europeans. Behind the bulldozers were the graders and
the steamrollers and the stamping gangs and behind them
all the bitumen plant, smoking and smelling of hot pitch.
They were working very rapidly. Another three months and
they would be through the town, out over the flats, and
linked up with the main north road. He started the car and
drove back to the house. He put the car away and latched
the garage door and walked slowly through the dusty garden. The wind was dropping. By nightfall it would be gone.
The town below was already in shadow. Some lights
twinkled in the mountain's shadow. He let himself in the
front door and put the cartridges on the hall table beside
the gunrack. He stood there for a few seconds, looking at
the guns, until his wife called out to him from the kitchen.
They were eating in the kitchen that night. Most evenings
they still ate in the front room, but on windy nights the
house became very cold after dark, because of its exposed
position, and they ate in the kitchen then, still warm from
the big wood stove. Gord preferred eating in the kitchen.
From the kitchen window he could see the thin screen of
young wattles he had planted three years ago and then the
empty bush stretching away to the mountains and the sea
beyond. On dark nights the lonely eye of a farmhouse light

in the blackness gleamed like the eye of a springhare, and on late summer evenings the sky over the mountains was a deep clear blue, touched with green, like water in a mountain lake when the snow is melting. And in the kitchen, the road gang, working late under floodlights, could hardly be heard.

They ate supper without talking much and then had their coffee in the nearly dark room. The room was still warm from the fire and the coals glowed through the open iron door, throwing a pool of red light on the stone floor. Afterwards he lit the lamp and they went through to the bedroom. He stopped in the hall and looked at the guns again, and the heads of leopard, buck, rhino, and the single mounted lion's head, the only lion's head he had kept, and he had shot twenty lions, not from a hide or a truck or an elephant's back, but standing on his own feet in the bush, as he had shot everything, elephant, rhino, sable, kudu, leopard, buffalo, never for the fun of shooting, but as a part of his job, or for food, or because they were killers, or marauders, but never for fun. There was a photograph on the wall near the guns, one of those old photographs which turn brown, of Gord standing beneath two elephant tusks which met over his head, and in those days he was nearly six feet two. They were the biggest tusks he had ever seen, probably a record for Tanganyika Territory, but that was during the war and he had shot the elephant to feed a whole kraal full of displaced Africans, and there was no time to worry about records. He had shot that bull with a heavy sporting rifle, a .400, in open country near a river; the bull had knelt down, balancing on its tusks, and then rolled over. It was a shot he was proud of because it had killed quietly and painlessly, but it was not a shot with any other merit attached to it, being neither tricky nor fast. But it had impressed the Africans and the young British infantry officer he was guiding. Thirty-five years ago he had been a very slim young man with a high forehead and long thin face and eyes which seemed too big for his head. In the photograph he was wearing army boots and puttees over khaki trousers and a Sam Browne over his brown shirt with ammunition in a pouch-belt. In the photograph he could see how his breast-pocket bulged with .400 ammunition.

"I was a fine young fellow, wasn't I?" he said, raising the lamp and letting the young man beneath the tusks look out into the hall.

"You're a fine old man," said his wife. She put her arm around him. "Come to bed, Gord. You're looking tired."

"Wasn't I a fine young man?" he asked. That must be the brandy, he thought, making me like this. One brandy. That shows what abstinence will do.

"Abstinence." he said to his wife, "Weakens a man. Living in a town weakens a man. But abstinence does it quicker."

"You're terribly tired," said his wife. "Please come to bed."

"Would you have fallen in love with me if I had not been such a fine young man?" he asked, moving the lamp around in front of the picture.

"I never knew you as a young man," she said.

"I was old and decrepit when you met me?" he said, but he was smiling now, because above all he did not want to make her unhappy, even when he felt like this. Suddenly, standing there, with the lamplight on the guns and the old photographs, the small brandy spent itself in him, running out of him like water spilt on sand, and he turned quickly and went into the bedroom. He undressed and got into bed, lying very tall and straight under the patchwork quilt. The wind had dropped and it was very quiet. The road gang had stopped for the night and in the wattles behind the house a nightjar was whistling.

6

He was with his brother again, in the bush beside the river, walking along the edge of the kloof, through the twisted spekboom; the slow river muddy brown. Below them the kloof, cool and shadowed green and brown. They stopped walking when they were hot and Gord sat on a low antheap. He was twenty-eight that year, just back from his first trip to Mozambique. They sat resting and looked across the kloof, two hundred yards wide here, rising gradually on the far bank, seamed with goat paths, patched with small thorn trees and occasional cactus. Down in the bush below them a monkey chattered a warning. The wind blew up the kloof, ruffling the river, shallow here, and stirring the bush. The river was the color of brandy over the white rocks. The river curled down among the low red hills to the sea. The tall yellow grass sang stiff in the wind on the hills. They sat and listened to the wind in the kloof.

"I wish a dassie'd come out," said his brother. Stuart was fifteen. "Would you shoot it, Gord? Reckon you'd hit it with that?"

Gord sat with the long Colt across his legs. It was an old

model, long-barreled, single-action, with a butt of carved stinkwood. It was his first handgun and he was very proud of it. He had bought it from a Portugese in Mozambique a year ago. All the way back, from Vila Fontes to Tete to Lourenço Marques to Ressano Garcia and up through the Lebombo Mountains to Johannesburg, he had taken lessons from anyone who could shoot a handgun, mainly policemen and gentlemen hunters. It had cost him a lot of money in ammunition. Not many people in Africa were good revolver shots, and he had become a celebrity on the transport train.

They sat watching the opposite bank. A small gray mouse-hawk was hovering just above the rim of the kloof, riding the breeze with short sweeps, his wings and tail fanned as he rose and fell on the stray eddies.

"They know he's waiting," said Stuart, pointing to the hawk.

"They won't come out while he's there. He's probably had a go at them already today."

The hawk went away down river in a long stiff-winged sweep. The black holes in the opposite bank stayed empty.

"They've had a scare all right," said Gord. He lifted the gun and squinted down the long barrel. The holes were eighty yards away, he reckoned. Fine for a .22 rifle, but much too far for a revolver. The sun was right overhead now and bright on the narrow ledges and tumbled stone around the holes. The hawk came back, flying low between the thorn trees, and settled on a dead tree above the dassie holes. He flapped his wings, teetering, then balanced himself and sat, shoulders hunched, watching the holes.

"*Give him a fright, Gord,*" *said Stuart.* "*Go on. Singe his feathers.*"

"*He's too far,*" *said Gord.* "*Hundred yards, at least.*"

"*Give him a fright,*" *said Stuart.* "*The dassies won't come out anyway while he's there.*"

Gord slid down the antheap and leaned against it, pulling his legs up in front of him and resting the barrel of the Colt on his knee.

He thumbed the big hammer, hearing with pleasure the deep strong well-oiled click as the gun cocked. The hawk was a tiny speck over the front sight.

The report made his ears sing and the hawk whirled down and away, flying low between the thorn bushes. He watched the hawk go and then he heard the sudden crashing stumble of a buck breaking cover in the kloof below him in a crackle of bursting bush and a clattering of small sharp hooves on loose stone.

"*Bushbuck,*" *shouted Stuart, on his feet now, excited.*

Fifty yards down the slope the thick bush shivered as something thrust through and then they heard the splash as the ram went through the shallow river, and the scrabbling of his hooves on the water-worn rocks as he scrambled up the other bank.

Then they saw him on the other side, running fast and frightened, his body low, a small dark shape among the thorn. Gord sat down again and thumbed the Colt and fired, too quickly, smiling at the jump of the heavy gun and the sharp powder smell and the high sweet buzzing in his ears. Slower, boy, he whispered softly, slower, and cool,

[31]

cool: only four left. He found the running buck again and put the gun high and ahead of it and —

Bowwww! *Red dust low.*

Bowwww! *Low dust again and the whine of a ricochet. He swung the long barrel, his ears buzzing now so that he could hear nothing but the buzzing, and took the gun in both hands, holding it down on his knee. The ram was past the hawk's tree now, out of the kloof, running on the flat, nearly two hundred yards —* bowwww! *The Colt jumped. Thumb hammer. Hold her down. Now oh please come on you bloody big dirty gun you big bloody dirty wonderful gun come on* bowwww! *and the ram was down, skidding in a little cloud of dust and the big Colt smoking and slightly warm on the chamber and his ears buzzing and his nose tingling with the cordite smell and he laid it in his lap and leaned back against the warm antheap, his hands trembling, looking at the gun lying there so innocent and inert now, with the small almost liquid trickle of smoke from the muzzle and the empty chambers. He shivered suddenly and ejected the empty shells one by one out onto the sand.*

"You'd better go'n get him," he said to Stuart.

"Hell," said the boy. "Bloody hell. What a fluke."

"Just you go'n get him," said Gord. He loaded the Colt. "Just you go'n get him."

Stuart ran down the kloof, whooping, his shirt flapping out of his trousers. Gord closed the gun and walked slowly after him. His stomach was fluttering slightly. When he was below the rim of the kloof he could no longer see the buck lying on the thorn flats across the river.

"It was a good shot," *he said aloud, as he went down the*

[32]

kloof, addressing himself to the bush around him. "It was a bloody good shot. You must admit it was a good shot."

Now thirty-odd years later he lay awake and still remembered it as a good shot, the best he had ever made. They still remembered it along the river. You could go to the hotel at the ferry and they'd walk you up the river a little and show you where Gord Vance shot the running buck with a Colt at two hundred yards in 1908. He went back there once, ten years before he moved into this house. The river was lower. The sandbar at the mouth had grown, and the river was reduced to a series of pools. The land on either side was cultivated now, lucerne on the side where he and Stuart had started the buck, and tall maize on the other bank. The wild thorn tree flats were all plowed under now and the maize stood tall and orderly, shimmering and rustling in the summer wind.

He lay in the dark and thought of the place as it had been and as it was now and then he thought of Stuart whom they had kept at Passchendaele, happy Stuart who was the worst shot Gord had ever seen. He wondered if the army had been able to teach Stuart to shoot. He doubted it. Shooting was one of those things. You either had a flair for it or you didn't. He guessed Stuart had died as he had lived, a bad shot who never cared. He was suddenly very sorry that he had not taken more time to teach his brother to shoot. Not that it would have made much difference, he thought. Men were easier to shoot than animals.

He went back to sleep finally and dreamed that he was

*sitting on the antheap above the river and watching the
tall maize across the kloof stir and ripple in the hot
wind.*

7

$\mathcal{T}$HE next day he put the Lee-Enfield in the Ford, laying it down on the torn back seat in its webbing case, and drove out to the farms along the river; the river dry now, the stones white and bleached in the sun. He slowed down at the railroad crossing and bumped across the rails, glancing quickly to left and right up the long shimmering steel as he went over. He was always afraid that a train would hit him, coming fast and roaring out of the bush.

Just over the crossing the empty hull of a small car lay on its side beneath a yellow-flowering mimosa tree. It had lain there, in sun, rain, and scouring sandy wind, for almost ten years. Gradually the human scavengers had picked it clean and now only the stark bare body shell remained, like the gutted carapace of a tortoise after a bush fire.

He looked at it now, as he clanked across the tracks, as he looked at it every time he passed this way, and remembered again old Tom Boshoff and the evening the southbound express had hit him. Tom was a real hell-raiser in those days, always on the drink, leaving his wife and children for days on end while he went whoring in the next town; he was the town's pet scandal. This night he was on his way to Aloes to pick up a girl for a weekend in Port Elizabeth. ("Christ, man," he would complain, years later, "I'd booked the bloody hotel room and everything, flowers and all.") There was a strong and noisy wind that evening, and Tom, with a few anticipatory brandies inside him, had driven fast through the bush in the windy dark without thinking of the train or hearing its long ululating whistle (and it had whistled, no doubt about that) and the south-bound, doing sixty through the dark, had clipped the back of the Volkswagen as it scuttled across, and flicked it fifty yards into the prickly pear. When they stopped the train and pried Tom out of the wreck he was unconscious and very nearly dead and the car smelled like a brewery, because the shock had made him vomit. In the emergency ward he regained consciousness on the operating table, just before they dropped the mask over his face, and felt the spew soaking his shirt.

"Oh God," he said, groaning and starting to cry, "I'm bleeding, hey?"

"If you are," said the doctor, who was irritable at being dragged out of bed at midnight, "it's Nelson's blood." As Tom said afterwards, he didn't think much of a doctor who couldn't tell brandy from rum.

But he was badly hurt. His skull was punched in, and his arm was broken, and the impact had put several verte-brae out of line. He was in the hospital for six months, a bitter, complaining patient, always half drunk on brandy his friends smuggled into him. When they discharged him, which must have been a great day for the hospital, he

could not taste or smell, and his memory was shot through
with great holes of forgetfulness. He was still on the com-
mittee of the local farmers' cooperative and sometimes it
was quite embarrassing when he stood up and started to
say something and then in the middle of it, right in the
middle of a sentence, he would forget what he wanted to
say and suddenly start off on something quite different, or
he would stand there without speaking, his face flushing
redder and redder, and then he would sit down and his
lips would move silently while he backtracked and tried
to remember what he'd started to say. Listening to Tom
was like listening to a radio with a loose wire: words came
through in bursts and crackles, unconnected, or sometimes
whole sentences would come through quite coherently and
everyone would relax and sit back and think: Well, this
time he's all right, he's going to get it out and we can get
on to the next item on the agenda; and then Tom would
stop, start, stutter, shoot out a few disconnected words, and
sit down.

But it was the loss of taste that annoyed him most. He
still smoked and ate as much as he ever did and drank
more, but to hear him you would think that he did these
things as a duty.

"This might's well be cow dung," he would say, eating
a steak in the private bar of the Royal, "for all the good
it is to me. And liquor might's well be horse-piss. I get no
pleasure out of eating or drinking anything now. Can't taste
nor smell anything, you don't know what it's like." He used
to get very sorry for himself on nights when he spoke like
this, and he used to put the brandy down at a great speed,

as though sheer quantity would jolt his taste buds back to life.

He had a metal plate in his skull and a broad scar where the hair never grew, like a fire break on a scrubby hill, and he had to wear a clumsy brace to stop his vertebrae jumping out of line, but it was this lack of taste and smell which pained him most.

His Volkswagen lay where the train had thrown it and gradually it seemed to become part of the surrounding bush. Grass grew up through the rents in the bodywork and the starred glass grew white and opaque. It was only in bad droughts, when the bush withdrew, that the wreck stuck out stark and inconguous, like a long-hidden wart in the thinning beard of an old man.

In the citrus plantations along the river the oranges were bright among the shining green leaves. Some fruit had fallen and lay on the cleared red earth beneath the trees. The trim orange trees stretched out, row and row, in straight neat lines to the hills ringing the valley. The lower hills were red, with dull green thorn and gray-green pale cactus on them: then they climbed more steeply, with dark green kloofs running up them, until they reared up high and blue against the sky.

Along the river the bush was still thick and green, tall trees hung with Spanish moss and leafy undergrowth, creepers and big flat-leaved succulents and maidenhair fern. The baboons came down through the kloofs and along the river bush and raided the fruit plantations. Gord drove along the river road and looked at the trees and thought that the baboons would probably be down that evening. They had not been down for some days, not in this part of the valley. If they came tonight he would be waiting for them. The farmers paid him a pound bounty for every baboon he shot. He picked up a jackal sometimes, and got the divisional council bounty on that, and sometimes he got a few dassies, but the baboons provided his regular income. They were clever animals and difficult to shoot and he had some admiration for them. He did not like shooting baboons or monkeys but it was the only way he could earn a living now, unless he wanted to become a weed picker and join the town council's squad of sad old pensioners. He drove along the river in the sun-bright morning and thought about the baboons again. Down here the road was shaded by the tall trees and the air was cool. There were ferns among the trees and they reminded him of the tall thick Kenya forests. Down in the river bed the sun on the white water-smooth rocks hurt his eyes.

He hoped the baboons might come through tonight. He could use a few pounds. He thought about baboons. Some people said they could count up to three. Some said they could count up to five. The figure varied, but it was generally agreed that they would know if three men went into a field and only two came out. They were difficult to lay for anyway, whether they could count or not. That did not worry Gord much. He had never relied much on blinds for shooting. He didn't like using blinds or beaters. If I can see it I can shoot it, he said, flexing his fingers on the wheel. Even now, with those blasted glasses, if I can see it I can shoot it. The glasses were new bifocals. He had only had them a few weeks and had done very little shooting with them, only a few rounds at a target down by the river. He knew that he was having a little difficulty in seeing the rear sight, but he told himself that once his eyes were used to the new glasses it would be all right.

The glasses were prim and rimless and made Gord look like a schoolmaster. He looked at himself in the rear-view mirror and frowned. He was worried about his eyes and he kept trying to convince himself that his sight was improving but he knew that it was not. What the devil, he thought resolutely, watching the road ahead and avoiding the bespectacled man in the mirror, what the hell, lots of people wear glasses these days, even kids at school, doesn't mean your sight's going just because you wear glasses. But he did not think he'd be much good with a revolver any more. He just had the feeling that he should not try anything with a revolver any more. Or an automatic. He had a good German automatic at home, a Mauser with a round wood-faced butt with a lanyard ring, a hammer-fired automatic with the square magazine in front of the trigger guard. It was a very heavy gun to carry but it felt good in your hand and shot accurately. The German army had issued them to officers, usually artillery officers, but Gord had taken his from a dead infantry officer in Tanganyika. He remembered now the young German with the neat mustache lying on the riverbank where the Vickers crew had caught him with a long burst as he ran for cover. His feet had slipped in the mud and the Vickers had stitched its pattern back and forth across his sweaty uniform before he could reach the bush. He remembered looking at the young man lying dead on the mud and thinking that the Vickers belt had probably been loaded by a pretty girl in an English factory, a girl like the ones in the Pear's Soap advertisements, pink-cheeked and curly-haired. Well, she'd got her German beast.

He drove across the dry drift, the Ford bouncing on the stones, and shifted into first to pull up the bank. The road on this side of the river was better. The big farmers lived up at this side of the river and they kept their roads in good shape. Gord drove along the good road between the plantations. The orange trees gave way to lemons. The trees with their smooth clean stems looked very civilized in the fresh morning. Somewhere among the trees a Christmas bee was buzzing and near the road a pair of red and black sunbirds were hovering around a cluster of late blossoms. Far away between the trees a yellow tractor was working.

He stopped at a gate two miles up the road. The last two miles had been through citrus plantations. Beyond the gate was the dark green of lucerne and beyond that he could see a small field of cabbages. Everything was very green and well tended. The gate was of wood beams, sanded and clear-varnished. On the side of the gate facing down the road was a neat wrought-iron sign, "Tharfield," and in smaller letters beneath it, but in a continuation of the same strip of iron, "J. D. Dickason." He opened the gate again and drove up to the house, through the avenue of young flowering gums. When he came out of the trees he saw cars parked in front of the dressed stone house, a new Ford and a Chevrolet Fleetline. They had Cape Town registration plates and they were both very dusty. The Chevrolet had a water bag hanging from its bumper. The water was sweating out of the bag and the dust on the canvas had turned to thin mud. He stopped the Ford and got out and he could smell the hot engines and he guessed they had been driven hard all the way from Cape Town.

A dog was barking behind the big house. The front door was open but the screen door was closed and Gord could not see inside. Then the screen door opened and J. D. Dickason came out. He was a big man without any fat or softness. His belly was big without being soft.

"Gord," he said. "Come up, man, come up." Two young men came out of the house, frowning in the morning glare, and watched Gord as he walked up the short green path to the stoep. Gord guessed the one was Dickason's boy. He looked like the old man. The other was a stranger.

Dickason sat down in a grass chair and hooked another out for Gord. The boys sat on the stoep railings, legs hanging down.

"You know my son?" said Dickason. "You remember Mr. Vance, Bobby? Yes? Good. Gord, this is a friend of Bobby's, Mr. Verster. Party of young people come up from Cape Town for the long weekend. God help innocent people on the roads."

"Did it in seven," said Bobby Dickason, looking at the Chevrolet.

"Haven't seen you for a long time, Bobby," said Gord. "Ten years, maybe. You're always away at school when I get around here."

"He's at the university now," said J. D. Dickason. "Doing

very well, too, eh, Bobby, when he stops chasing the girls."

Another young man came out of the house. He was wearing very short blue shorts and a blue-and-white shirt and sandals. He was carrying a .22 rifle and a shotgun. He leaned them against the railings.

"This is another of them," said J. D. Dickason. "House is full of them. Harry, this is Mr. Vance. Gord, Mr. Mulder."

The young man nodded. "How do you do." He was not very interested in Gord. Somewhere back in the house a young girl laughed and laughed. Gord reckoned there must be quite a crowd in there.

"Came up to have a go at the *bobbejane*," said Gord. "Your fruit looks good. Just wanted to let you know before I went into the kloof."

"Well," said J. D. Dickason. He stood up and looked out across the valley. "Well, Gord, these youngsters have come up just for that. Come up for the weekend to have a go at the baboons. Of course"— trying to joke —"of course, the baboons are quite safe. Not like having a real shot after them."

"That's all right," said Gord. He felt himself flushing. Damn it. "That's all right. Just thought of it this morning, that's all. Just thought I'd take a spin out."

"Pity you didn't ring," said Dickason. "Pity you didn't give me a tinkle. Saved you the trouble of driving up."

"It doesn't matter," said Gord. The young men were looking away. His being there annoyed and embarrassed them and he wanted to get away himself.

"Why don't you go with them?" said Dickason. "Teach them how to shoot, hey?"

"Yes, come along, Mr. Vance," said Bobby. He spoke without any enthusiasm. In the house the girl laughed again. It was getting hot on the stoep now and Gord felt the perspiration in the small of his back. There was a thin film of sweat on his glasses.

"Thanks," he said, "but I'll go on down the valley. Couldn't keep up with you in the hills. Getting past it." He smiled and his face felt terrible.

He did not want them to see his disappointment. He smiled again and stood up. Down in the valley the long rows of orange and lemon trees were beginning to waver in the heat. Down on the main road a truck passed and the dust drifted slowly across the dark green trees. Somewhere a crow was calling loudly, complainingly. On the freshly watered strip of lawn below the stoep a black-and-orange hoopoe was probing the soil for worms, fanning and closing its crest as it hunted among the grass roots.

"It's quite all right," he said again. "No trouble at all. It doesn't matter."

But of course it did matter very much. He said goodbye and walked down the path to the old Ford, walking very erect, feeling the clips of new .303 ammunition in the side pockets of his old coat, and he knew it mattered very much. Just feeling the ammunition bumping against his hips as he walked reminded him that it mattered very much. He opened the door and as he sat down on the hot leather his knee gave a twinge and he winced.

His kneecap had been removed many years before and it ached if he walked much, but he had not walked much today and it had no right to be aching now. He sat there

for a minute, fumbling with the ignition key without seeing
it, with his other hand rubbing his knee. On the keyring at
home he had a mushroomed .455 revolver bullet which they
had taken out of him after it had smashed his knee and gone
on down to splinter the two lower leg bones. The lead
bullet was quite misshapen. It had been fired from an army
model Webley at about three feet and had done consider-
able damage.

He started the car and drove slowly down the road.
J. D. Dickason waved from the stoep and Gord stuck his
arm out of the window and waved back to show there
were no hard feelings. The young men did not wave. It's
his land, thought Gord. He stopped for the gate and opened
it and drove through, leaving the Ford's engine running
while he got out to close it again. His leg was still aching
and the limp that came and went was back again. It's his
land and if he wants his boy and his friends to hunt on it,
well, that's his business. But I could have done with a few
quid. He felt the ammunition clips in his pocket and
thought that he could really have used a few quid. He felt
some resentment because the youngsters were only out for
fun but he realized that it was really Dickason's land and
he had no right to feel that way; he should feel grateful
for the times Dickason had let him use the land. But they
would not shoot anything, he knew, except perhaps a hare
or a monkey or a ringtail cat started by the dogs, and while
they were doing this they'd chase everything else back into
the hills for days. They'd take their girls with them and
they'd shoot at anything that moved and they'd have a
braaivleis and it would be like marching a regiment through

[45]

the bush, they and their toy rifles and pedigreed dogs that
would get killed by the first bush pig they put up. It wasn't
any of his business. He drove through the drift along the
river road under the trees. The sun was overhead now and
the sunlight shafting down through the leaves into the dark
places of the kloofs. He laid his leg across the driveshaft
tunnel so that the knee was not bent and after a while the
ache faded.

8

The bar had earth walls and a corrugated-iron roof and held the day's heat like an oven. The double doors were open and from the bar you could see the dusty road and the limp banana palms and up the road a way the bright red flame tree flowers.

A long wagon was parked under the flame trees. The team had been outspannead and the disselboom stuck out into the sunlight. The wheels were very shiny where the brake shoes had gripped them. They were the only things about the wagon which looked new. The rest was worn and sun-cracked and dusty.

Gord stood at the bar and drank a small beer. The wagon driver was drinking with friends in the corner. They were all drunk and getting noisy. It was five in the afternoon and there was a stale wind from the south, flat and un-pleasant as an invalid's breath. Through the window behind the bar Gord could see a big mango tree. There were some small green mangos among the leaves. The thick dusty leaves stirred slackly in the wind.

The transport driver came up to the bar and ordered

*some more drinks. The Portuguese storekeeper came out of
the room behind the bar and served him.*

*"You have one?" said the transport driver. He was talking
to Gord. "Join us. A beer for this gentleman, please. Un
cerveja, obbrigado."*

*Gord poured the beer into his glass. The bottle was warm
to the touch and the beer frothed up and ran down the
sides of the glass.*

*"Sorry, sorry," said the storekeeper. He wiped the beer
off the counter and the glass and went back to the room
behind the bar. Gord picked up the beer and walked across
to the transport driver and his team. He would have preferred not to drink with them, but there it was. The wagon
driver was a small man with one blind eye. It was a smoky
blue with a white spot where the pupil should have been.
He and his team had just come through from Swaziland.
The roads had been bad after the rains and they had had a
rough trip.*

*"The road's pretty good from here to the Bay," said Gord.
They called Lourenço Marques the Bay, meaning Delagoa
Bay, but its real name was Lourenço Marques Bay.*

"You just come up?" said the driver. "Cheers."

*"Yes," said Gord. He was waiting for a wagon going
through to Pretoria. He had spent six months in Mozambique and he wanted to get back to South Africa for a while.*

"Same again?" said the driver. He stood up.

*"It's mine," said Gord. He felt in his pockets and hoped
he had enough money. He never could work out prices in
escudos. He looked at the driver's friends. They were leaning back in their chairs. One had his hat over his face. The*

other was snoring softly. They had not spoken since Gord joined the table.

"They're out," said the driver. Gord ordered two more beers. The driver nodded at his friends.

"They had a rough trip."

"Looks like it," said Gord.

Down the road they heard a wagon approaching. They walked outside and watched it come. It pulled in under the flame trees and they watched while the team was outspanned by the driver, an old African, and a very small boy. It was an open flat-top wagon with small packing cases lashed to it. Two white men had been sitting on the tailboard. When the oxen were unspanned the white men spoke to the African and his boy and then walked across to the bar. The men were about the same age, in their thirties. One was wearing dark brown corduroy trousers and velskoens without socks and a dark green shirt. The other was wearing khaki trousers and army boots and an army shirt with shoulder loops. They looked very tired. When they took their floppy hats off there were hard lines above their eyes where the sunburn ended.

"Hot trip," said Gord's driver.

"Yes," said the green-shirted one. They went into the bar and sat at a table in the far corner. The storekeeper came out and they ordered beers and fish and vegetables. They put their hats on the floor and drank their beer. When the food came they started eating immediately, ordering more beer. The driver and Gord came back inside. The driver stood at the bar near the newcomers' table. They ate without looking at him. Gord sat down at the table. He felt like

a fool sitting at the table with the two sleeping drunks, but he was tired of the driver's company and did not want to stand at the bar with him.

"Where from?" asked the driver. He was beginning to have a little difficulty with his speech. "Where you just from?"

The army-shirted one looked at him. He finished chewing before he spoke, which Gord thought was an unnecessarily polite gesture.

"The Bay," he said.

"Road all right?" asked the driver. He moved closer along the bar. He wanted this conversation to keep going.

"Not bad," said the army-shirt.

"Man here says it's pretty good," said the driver, indicating Gord. The army-shirt man looked at Gord and then looked away.

"Not bad," he said. "It's all right."

"He said it was pretty good," said the driver. He bought another beer and came closer.

"Hey. Have a beer, hey?" He wanted to keep this fascinating conversation going.

The army-shirt looked at him.

"All right," he said.

"All right," said the green-shirt. The driver rapped on the counter and the storekeeper came out. The driver bought three more beers. He had lost interest in Gord. The newcomers were so talkative.

It was very hot in the bar. The wind had risen a little and was blowing sand down the road. Under the flame trees the Africans were cooking over a small fire. Gord could smell the wood smoke when the wind veered. He looked at the men drinking with the driver and wondered if he should touch them for a ride across the border. Perhaps they would need help in the mountains. It looked like they only had one old kaffir and a picannin. He walked over to the bar and knocked on it. The storekeeper came out of the back and gave him another beer. The storekeeper was suffering conflicting emotions. He wanted his afternoon sleep but he also wanted to take advantage of this unusual activity in his bar on a weekday afternoon. Gord picked up his beer and walked across to the table. He stood beside the driver. The driver looked up.

"My friend," he said. "My old friend. Meet my new friends." He waved his hand.

"You going through tonight?" asked Gord. The men looked at him. They looked at his patched trousers and the ammunition clips on his belt and straw hat.

"Perhaps," said the green-shirt, very carefully.

"Chance of a lift?" asked Gord.

"How'd you get here?" asked the army-shirt. He looked at Gord again. "Why didn't you go back like you came? We don't want to pick up no hoboes."

"I was stuck here," said Gord. To hell with them, he thought. I don't have to tell them anything.

"He looks all right," said green-shirt.

"You got to be careful," said army-shirt.

"He looks all right," said green-shirt. "Sit down. Name's Walt. This's Trev."

"No offense," said Trev. "You just got to be careful who you pick up, you know."

[51]

"*I know,*" *said Gord.*

"*Wagon was held up last month,*" *said Trev.* "*Some fellow they'd picked up in Komatipoort. Waited till they were in the kloofs and then held them up and came across here.*"

"*I didn't hear about it,*" *said Gord.* "*I've been up the coast.*"

"*Wouldn't get away with it 'f it was me,*" *said the driver.* "*I'd fix the bastard all right.*"

He stood up and pushed his chair away from the table and walked out into the sunlight. He was staggering a little.

"*He's had enough,*" *said Walt.*

"*When you going through?*" *asked Gord.*

"*Tomorrow morning, early. You're welcome,*" *said Trev.* "*Sorry I was funny before. You just got to be careful. You got a gun?*"

"*Yes,*" *said Gord. His rifle was with his horse, under the trees.*

"*It helps,*" *said Trev.* "*Just in case. You never can tell. It's good to have an extra gun just in case.*"

The driver came back inside. His face was sweating from the walk in the sun. When he came in the door the light was behind him and they could not see what he was carrying. Then he came around the table and stood in front of them with the light from the door on him and they saw he was holding a great big army model Webley .455 with the hammer back.

"*Hey,*" *said Trev, annoyed.* "*Hey. Stop playing with that.*"

The big gun was jerking around in the driver's hand.

[52]

"I'm ready for thim" he said. "Ready for any of thim. Jus' let thim try me. I'll show bastards."

He swung the revolver so that it pointed at Gord. Gord stood very still. The muzzle of the big Webley was a black hole and he could see the blunt tips of the unjacketed bullets in the chambers.

"You okay?" he asked Gord. "How we know you okay. You jus' walk in here. How we know you okay?"

"He's all right," said Walt.

"Of course." said Trev. "Put that thing away before we have an accident!"

They had all sobered up very quickly. All except the driver. The two drunks in the corner had woken and were watching. One of them called out, "Hey, what's trouble, hey?" But nobody took any notice. The storekeeper leaned over the counter and said, "No guns in my place, senhors, no guns in my place, hey please." A woman came out of the back room and gave a little scream.

"Come on," said Trev. "Have a drink." He stood up and reached for the Webley. "Put that down and have a drink, old man. Come on, old man."

The driver backed away. He swung the revolver and staggered a little.

"Nobody touches my gun. This is my gun."

"That's all right," said Walt. "Just put it down and we'll have a drink, hey?"

"Come on, old man," said Trev. The driver backed away. Gord stood up and walked across to Trev. He was tired of the driver.

"*Oh, put it down,*" *he said.* "*Here, let me hang on to it for you.*" *He stepped forward.*

"*I'll do it,*" *said the driver.* "*I'll keep it.*" *He wrapped his thumb around the hammer, holding it, and squeezed the trigger. The Webley made a monstrous report in the small shed. Gord lay on the dusty boards and looked at the smoking Webley. He was violently angry. There was blood on the knee of his khaki trousers and he could feel it running down his leg.*

"*I'm sorry,*" *said the driver.* "*I'm sorry, I'm sorry, I'm sorry. It just went off. I was uncocking it and it just went off. I was just uncocking it and it went off.*"

Gord moved his leg and the first delicate tentacle of pain touched his mind and went away again.

"*For Christ's sake take it away from him before he shoots me again,*" *he said.*

Trev took the Webley from the driver and knelt down beside Gord. The Portuguese storekeeper came around the counter with his wife.

"*Get him out of here,*" *he kept saying. He meant the driver.*

"*Get him out of here and get the* policia. *Policia, policia, get the* policia."

"*Bugger the* policia," *said Walt.* "*Where's the doctor?*"

"*I didn't mean it,*" *said the driver.* "*As God is my witness, I didn't mean it. It just went off. I was uncocking it.*"

"*Shut up, you booze artist,*" *said Walt. He knelt down and pulled Gord's trouser leg up. Just about the knee there was a small dark hole, bluish at the edges. The blood was swelling out of it slowly and steadily. There was a small pool on the floor already.*

"It's not bleeding bad," said Trev with great authority. "It's not bleeding bad. The main artery's not cut."

"How would you know?" said Gord. He was frightened now. He knew what a big lead bullet could do. He was frightened at the thought of the damage to the bones of his leg and he was afraid that the pain would return before they got him to a doctor. I'm no hero, he thought. Not in cold blood like this.

"Can you get a doctor?" he asked.

"I think we should get a doctor," said Walt.

"Yes. But there's no danger. The artery's not cut," said Trev. "We have plenty of time." He was enjoying himself.

"WILL YOU BLOODY PLEASE FOR CHRIST'S SAKE GET ME TO A DOCTOR?" shouted Gord.

The Portuguese storekeeper came back with a customs officer and a policeman. He had fetched them from the border post.

"Is there a charge?" asked the policeman. He looked at the blood on the floor with academic interest.

"You are all right? There is a charge?"

"Is no doctor," said the storekeeper. "He's go back to Lourenço Marques."

"He was only for the day," said the customs man informatively. "Thursdays he is only for the day. Every Thursday he is here, but for the day only."

"Just making calls," said the storekeeper helpfully.

"Yes, calls," said the customs man, delighted at this addi-

tion to his English vocabulary. "On Thursdays, but just for calls."

The storekeeper's wife wrapped Gord's leg in strips of clean cloth. The blood seeped through immediately. Gord began to get worried. The woman brought an old sheet and tore strips of cloth from it. Gord guessed she was worried about her floor.

"Where is the man with the gun?" asked the policeman.

"Here is the gun," said Trev. The policeman took the gun and held it by the trigger guard.

"The man is outside at the wagons," said the storekeeper.

"Drunken bastard," said Walt.

"What is his nationality?" asked the policeman.

"What's the difference?" said Trev.

"It is important," said the policeman.

"South African, I guess," said Walt. "I think so."

"It can make trouble," said the policeman.

"I have seen his passport," said the customs officer. "He is South Africano."

"I shall arrest him," said the policeman with decision. He went outside. The customs officer followed him.

The woman brought a blanket and covered Gord, tucking it under his feet and along his body.

"For shock," said Trev. "You musn't get cold."

"That stupid bugger," said Walt. "How could he be such a stupid bugger?"

"How does it feel?" asked Trev.

"It's all right," said Gord. There was no pain at all, just the dampness of the blood soaking the bandages. He lay

very still, waiting for the pain to start and hoping it would stay away until they got him to a doctor.

The storekeeper and the policeman came back inside. "We are taking you to the Bay," said the storekeeper. "We are using that man's wagon.

"The man who shot you," said the policeman. "I have allowed it. I take responsibility."

They put him on the wagon and when it was harnessed they drove through Lourenço Marques. He slept most of the way and when he woke it was the next morning. His leg was stiff and throbbing regularly. It was a bright morning but there was a breeze off the sea and the wide streets under the flame trees were still cool.

By the time they reached the hospital he was feverish. His head ached and he could not think straight. He groaned a little when they put him on a stretcher and carried him into the hospital. The customs officer had driven down with them and he spoke to the duty doctor. The duty doctor was a small trim Portuguese. He examined the wound and spoke to the customs officer.

"He says it is bad," said the customs officer. "He must operate."

Two orderlies came out and carried Gord through the administration block of the hospital to the casualty theater. They walked across a tidy quadrangle of red gravel fringed with lawns and a hibiscus hedge.

In the theater the orderlies washed and shaved the leg. The customs officer was very interested. The doctor put on a clean gown and a mask. They wheeled Gord into the operating theater. Through the window he could see the *bright gardens and the red-roofed wards beyond the gardens. An old man in a wheel-chair was propelling himself slowly along the gravel path.*

A second doctor came in. He was wearing a mask and a gown and all Gord could see were his eyes and a bald head. He wheeled a small table up to the operating table and Gord smelled alcohol and chloroform. The customs officer came in with the first doctor and shook Gord's hand.

"I go now," he said. "You will be all right. I have told them to look after you very well. You will be all right. I must go now to return the wagon to Ressano Garcia and also take up my duties."

"Thank you very much," said Gord.

The doctor said something long and involved.

"He says he will try to save the leg," said the customs officer. "He says he will do all he can to save the leg."

"Tell him I want the bullet," said Gord.

"I will tell him," said the customs man. "He says he will do all he can to save the leg. It may remain stiff, but he will try to save it."

The customs officer spoke to the doctor and turned to go. The anesthetist picked up the mask and stood beside the table and said something to the customs officer, who turned at the door.

"He wants to know," he said to Gord, "do you know Mister Piet Bosch? He is a South Africano."

"No," said Gord. The smell of ether was very strong and his head was starting to swim and he felt sick.

"No. Why?"

"He is there," said the customs officer. He pointed across

[58]

the theater. Against the wall was a trolley with a sheet
covering something on it. The sheet was not quite long
enough and a pair of dusty boots stuck out.

"He had an accident," said the customs officer. "The
authorities want to find his relations. He had an accident
in the street last night. You don't know him? That is a
shame."

He smiled and went out, leaving the door open. Gord was
still looking at the corpse when the anesthetist put the
mask over his face.

9

*R*EMEMBERING, he smiled and fingered the place where the kneecap had been. That dago doc had done a good job. It had taken a long time, but he had done a good job. The wound had gone bad and they had opened it up again, picking out a lot of splintered bone from the lower leg. Then it had seized up tight, so that he could not bend it at all, and they had talked of amputating it. He had fought that and they had discharged him with it stiff. The doctor was glad he had saved it but was very apologetic about the stiffness. He had written a complete description of the operation in Portuguese for the South African doctors who might have to reopen the leg, and he had given this and some very artistic pen-and-ink drawings of the operation to Gord. They were good sketches. The leg bones were in black ink and the incisions were marked in red. Gord still had them.

The leg had slowly limbered up until he had almost full use of it. He was never again as active as he had been, but at least he had a leg he could use.

He had come back to the Transvaal with a few pounds

in his pocket and a mushroomed .455 bullet and taken it
easy for a year, working as a foreman-gardener on a mine
owner's estate north of Johannesburg.

He drove along the river road and wondered which farm
he should try next. J. D. Dickason's farm was the best. The
main kloof coming down from the mountains opened out
into his land. If only the kids had not come up. He felt
suddenly very bitter. Remembering Mozambique had hurt
him, he knew. Now he was susceptible to hurt and he did
not want to be hurt. He decided that he could not face any
more young people that day. In any case, he told himself,
in any case, once young Dickason's crowd get into the hills,
there'll be nothing for miles. It would have been fine if I
could have covered Dickason's orchard from along the
river and waited for baboons to come through this afternoon. But with my leg acting up I'm no good for spooring
anything through the bush. He took the ammunition clips
out of his pocket and put them in the glove box. In the
glove box were the sandwiches Julia had made him and a
Thermos of coffee. He pulled the Ford off the road and
drove in under some boerboon trees and stopped. He got
out and sat on the Ford's wide running board and un-
wrapped the sandwiches and poured some coffee into the
tin cup of the Thermos.

The grass was long under the trees and there was a
trickle of water in the river here, just enough to form small
pools among the rocks. In the trees over the river weaver
birds were nesting. He sat and watched them. Their nests
were kidney-shaped with a long entrance funnel. They

[61]

were carefully plaited with grass. Some of the nests were
very new. He could see that by the grass, which was still
green. Others were yellow and brown. Down on the stones
near a small pool a hamerkop bird was standing, watching
something in the shallow water. The hamerkop was a dark
brown with a crest of feathers jutting behind his head. He
looked very sleek and self-satisfied and was not really
interested in whatever was moving in the pool. He's probably just eaten, thought Gord, watching him. Probably
found some redfins trapped in the rocks and gorged
himself. They were birds that gorged themselves. They
made huge untidy nests of sticks and grass high up in thorn
trees, nests that looked strong enough to hold a man, huge
ragged rafts balanced in the trees. The hamerkop became
bored and flapped slowly down the river, flying low and
keeping in the shadow of the trees. Gord sat and watched
the water spiders skating on the still amber water. He
wondered if there were any trout in the river. The provincial
administration had tried to stock the river once but the
water level was very erratic, and the year after the stocking,
which was done up in the mountains, there had been a bad
drought. The trout were rainbow and reputedly very tough
and adaptable and quite suitable for this river, but the
provincial administration had put five thousand fingerlings
in and nobody had ever seen one since the day they were
taken up into the mountains. Other rivers had been stocked
successfully, but this was one of the failures.

He finished the sandwiches and the coffee and was going
to wash the Thermos in the river when he remembered that

the river was supposed to have the bilharzia snail here in the lower reaches. He put the Thermos back in the glove box and backed the Ford out from under the trees and drove home.

10

*U*p in the hills J. D. Dickason's boy Bobby had shot a hornbill. The clumsy big-beaked bird had just finished walling up his mate in a hollow tree with her eggs. He had walled her up with mud, leaving a hole big enough for his beak when he brought her food. He was digging grubs out of a rotting boerborn tree when Bobby and his friends came out of the kloof and Bobby shot him with the .22, a really wonderful shot, a bird as big as a turkey at thirty yards. The hollow-point bullet had gone right through the hornbill and now the bird lay with his wings fanned in the grass.

"What is it?" asked one of the girls.

"I don't know," said Bobby, "but it looks dangerous." He turned the hornbill over with his foot. The hornbill was a young cock in its third season, with his first and only mate walled up in a hollow tree, waiting for him to come and feed her.

One of the boys picked the bird up, hefting it.

"He's a good weight," he said. Then they all hefted it in turn.

"Well, he won't take any more chickens," said one of the boys, authoritatively. He thought the hornbill was a hawk. Only a hawk could have a beak like that.

"We going to keep it?" asked one of the girls. She looked at it with distaste. "To eat?"

"No," said Bobby. "He's a junk-eater. We'll leave it for some kaffir to find. Come on."

They walked on up the hill. The breeze came down from the hills and ruffled the hornbill's feathers.

11

On a bright day a week later Gord sat on the stoep and drank coffee and watched the road gang. They were getting closer every day. It was a cool morning and the air was very clear. The mountains were very blue, with the kloofs and poorts dark creases on them. I wish I were in the mountains, he thought. Just me alone. Like in the old days. He looked at his wife and felt sudden resentment and then he felt guilty because of the resentment. He had no reason to feel resentment or anything but love and deep gratitude for her. He was suddenly glad that he was not alone. A minute before he was wishing he was. Now he knew that he was frightened of being alone and did not want to be alone.

"I'm going into town," he said. "Anything you want?"

"No," she said. "I've got everything we need. Have another cup of coffee before you go. It's still hot."

She poured him another cup and they sat on the stoep in the sun, looking out over the valley. Her face was very peaceful and remarkably smooth for her age. There were

many fine wrinkles around her eyes but her cheeks and
forehead and chin were smooth and brown.

"You might get me some thread," she said. "I've just
remembered I want to patch that old blue dress of mine.
I might as well use it about the house. Light blue."

"I'll get it," he said. "Don't keep lunch for me. I want
to see some people."

"Please have something to eat," she said. "Please, Gord.
It's terribly bad for you. You must eat regularly."

"Don't you want to come down for the drive?" he asked.
We can have lunch down there, one of the cafés or the
railway buffet."

She shook her head.

"I've got a lot to do, Gord," she said.

"You don't get out much, Julia. You should come. You
need a break."

"I don't mind, really. I'm happy at home, Gord."

"At home," he said. He laughed and stood up. "At home.
I suppose it's a home."

She looked at him without smiling, but without anger or
worry or envy. "It's my home, Gord. It's a fine home. I've
never had a home like it. I don't want it any different."

"You've had a fine life," he said, suddenly feeling very
bitter. "You've had a fine, full, interesting life with me,
haven't you?"

She looked at him and smiled.

"I've had a fine life, Gord. I thank God every night for
my life. I've never wanted for anything. I was happy when
I married you and I'm happy now. It's been a fine life and
I'm very grateful."

"I've given you nothing," he said. "Nothing. Not even a family. You always wanted a family."

"When I was a girl, yes. But I wasn't a girl when I married you. I was a woman. A middle-aged woman. I didn't want anything except you then and now I'm an old woman and I don't want anything else. I don't want a family or another house or a new car or anything, anything at all."

He kissed her goodbye then and she stood on the stoep and watched him back the Ford out of the shed and bump down the road.

She stood with her hands on the stoep railings and watched him go. I wish he wouldn't worry so, she thought. He does worry, all the time. She hated to think of him worrying about her. Their debts and their poverty worried her only because of the effect they had on him. She did not feel like that at all. She had everything she wanted from life; indeed, more than she had ever expected. She wished Gord could see that.

She sighed and went inside. In the dim cool hall the serious young man under the two arched elephant tusks looked steadily at her. She touched the picture gently with one finger.

"Oh Gord," she said.

12

*H*is father had been a British infantry officer. He had come out during the Zulu wars of the 'seventies. After the fighting he had taken his discharge in South Africa and used his gratuity to buy a small farm on the Bobbejaan River in the Eastern Cape.

He was a tall, dignified man with thick white hair and a long white beard. He always regarded himself as an officer and a gentleman. He disciplined his family very strictly but it was a discipline of mutual courtesy rather than force. Right up to the day of his death at ninety-one he insisted that his sons wear jackets to the table.

He was a very competent if unimaginative artist in the traditional Victorian manner (still lifes, animals at bay, vaguely Jewish beauties loitering beside melancholy woodland pools, Redcoats beleaguered by painted savages) and as he grew older he painted more and farmed less, so that the heavy mortgage on the farm was never paid off.

In the last year of his life he became convinced that he could improve on the work of his younger years. His eyes were very bad by then and his hands shook and all his *judgment had gone and a great many pictures were ruined. He also took to gouging out the eyes of his portraits, probably because his own eyes were failing rapidly. The family hid as many of his pictures as they could, but he found most of them, prowling through the house in the early morning, and very few escaped. One of the best that survived, a sensitive charcoal drawing of a lion's head, was given to Gord after the old man's death.*

The old man had loved Africa and animals and the bush but had never really been a bushman. He was rather like the sailor who spends forty years at sea and never learns to swim.

After his death the farm was sold and the family split up. Gord's mother had gone to live with a married sister in Cape Town. His mother was a quiet, God-fearing woman without any impact. In the colorless suburb, among the drab gardens and low dark houses with red iron roofs and elaborately timbered stoeps, she had slowly faded away, becoming less and less real, so that when news of her death reached him in Tanganyika, Gord had the feeling that she had died years before. She had, for him.

His brother Arthur had gone to Rhodesia, sweated a living for years, and then gone into tobacco farming and died rich. The youngest brother, Clifford, had died of some vague African disease in Nigeria. Gord's sister, Dolly, had married a farmer in the Langkloof, the beautiful valley in the Tzitzikama Mountains. Gord had visited them twice, the first time for a weekend, and the second, after his first trip to Mozambique, for a month.

He and Dolly's husband, Lance, got on very well. Lance

was a serious, quiet man. He was a very good shot and had shot for South Africa in the 1920 Bisley match. He had a beautiful rifle, an 1890 model Winchester pump-action, with a long octagonal barrel and a straight, long wooden stock. It had leaf sights and the pump-action cocked a hammer with a complicated breechblock action. It was an accurate rifle and could be fired very rapidly. Lance seldom hunted, but he used the rifle to shoot the occasional hare or pheasant for the pot, usually shooting over the top of the windshield of the old Model A Ford he drove into the village, Misgund Oos, on Friday shopping trips. He kept the Winchester in the corner of the bedroom, ready for marauding hawks or for knocking off the red-winged spreeuws which fouled the rain water tanks. He also shot the crows which scratched in the mealie field across the valley. It was a good two hundred yards but he seldom missed. While Gord was staying with them he and Lance used to sit on the stoep in the cool twilight with a bottle of brandy, a jug of water, the Winchester and a box of cartridges, and wait for the guinea fowl to come foraging in the freshly planted field.

After Gord's last visit Lance came out onto the stoep one summer afternoon and saw a black head bobbing up and down in a furrow. He went back inside and got the Winchester and steadied it against the stoep railing and waited for the crow to bob up again. His first shot clipped red dust from the sods beside the head. He jacked another bullet into the chamber and was just going to fire again when the little African toddler, whose mother had left him to play in the furrow while she picked prickly pears be-

side the field, stood up. Lance walked back inside and put the gun in the corner and never touched it again. Gord was told the story years later. He still laughed when he thought of Lance's face when the piccanin stood up.

With age Lance had become even more serious. He did very little work on the farm now, just a little pottering around in the garden, a stooped elderly man with a soft face and thin gray hair. Most afternoons he slept. In the evenings he would sit on the stoep until it was dark, looking out over the valley. There was a big fir tree just below the house, the only one in the district.

Lance's first car was parked beneath it. It was an old touring Rover with a high slab-sided body and wooden-spoked artillery wheels. It had stopped running years ago and Lance had finally given up trying to get it going again. The wheels had sunk into the ground a little and there were pine needles rotting on the seats and piled on the bonnet and the windscreen was an opaque, cloudy yellow-white.

The starting crank was still in the radiator where Lance had left it in anger twenty years before.

13

*I*N the town the water cart had just damped the streets
to lay the dust and the air was still fresh. Gord parked the
Ford and walked along the pavement to the Royal Hotel.
The bars had just opened and in the lounge a servant was
pouring fresh sea sand into the fire buckets. The bar had
been swept and the counter polished and the barman was
slicing lemon on a scarred board, cutting the lemon into
very thin slices and skewering the slices on toothpicks. The
Royal was a respectable hotel and you always got a slice
of lemon with your gin-and tonic without having to ask
for it.

He sat at the bar. The wood was still damp. The bar
smelled faintly of soap and disinfectant and very slightly
of stale liquor. The barman finished slicing the lemon and
turned to Gord, wiping his hands on a towel.

"Yes," he said, "good morning." He was a young Afrikaner on holiday relief duty at the hotel. He did not know
any of the customers by name yet. In his first few days
there he had tried to get friendly but he had not been very
successful, mainly because his jokes and wisecracks were

Johannesburg jokes, and this town was a long way from
Johannesburg or indeed any big town. So now he just
served the drinks and marked off the days on a calendar
behind the bar. He couldn't wait to get back to the city.

"Beer, please," said Gord.

"Shelf or forty-five?" asked the barman.

"Pardon?" said Gord.

"Shelf or forty-five?" said the barman again.

"Cold," said Gord. "I mean cold. Sorry."

The barman took a beer out of the cooling shelf and
jerked the cap off. A small white peak of foam came out of
the neck of the brown bottle. The barman took a glass
off the rack, wiped it with the towel he had used for his
hands, and poured an inch of beer into it, tilting the glass.
He put the glass and the bottle on the counter in front of
Gord.

"That's forty-five. Forty-five's cold, hey? That's the temperature, hey?"

"I see," said Gord. "Thank you."

Here, thought the barman. *Here,* save me from this.
Roll on the thirtieth. He went back to slicing lemons. The
Royal did big business in gin-and-tonics on Wednesdays,
when the Rotary Club held its weekly luncheon in the
Royal Buffet and Grill Room upstairs.

Gord drank his beer slowly. He had never been a heavy
drinker and even now, at sixty-nine, he felt vaguely guilty
when he drank alone in a public bar. This bar, like most
South African public bars, was quite anonymous. The
counter was long and clean. The ashtrays had been donated
by the Du Maurier cigarette company. Instead of a bar rail

there was a shallow concrete trough which served as a foot-rail, spittoon, and ashtray. The long mirror behind the bar was just starting to turn yellow at the edges. Overhead a big-blade fan flicked slowly and uselessly. In the summer it became very hot in the bar and the open-front cooling shelves had no effect at all. Gord made his beer last an hour. He was putting off going out into the street. At noon two young farmers dressed in their town suits came in. They ordered brandy-and-waters and stood at the counter. Their suits were ten years out of date. Gord had not bought a new suit for more than ten years, but he read the news-papers and he knew what was being worn. He guessed these farmers had come in for the Rotary luncheon, prob-ably as guests. Funny how you can tell a farmer a mile off, he thought, looking at them. Doesn't matter whether he's big or little, whether he went to agricultural college or whether he grubbed up the hard way, you can tell one a mile off.

He sat watching them without really seeing them. He was thinking how much he had wanted to be a farmer. He should have gone up to Rhodesia when land was cheap and he'd have been rich by now, probably retired and having a vacation overseas every year, or running a little fruit farm down in the Cape. But we do things when we're young because we want to have the fun then, not thirty years later, so we go shooting and hellcatting and just plain bushwhacking up in Mozambique and the Lowveld and then civilisation and old age catch us together and land us in a Godforsaken little dorp which has all the vices and few of the advantages of civilization, surrounded by open country which is emasculated by fences and barbed wire and roads and boundaries and telegraph wires and railway tracks. Some of the farmers in the district, after shooting out all the wild game, were breeding herds of springbok and blesbok. They were tame as goats and the annual shoot was like a day at a rifle range. He felt suddenly more depressed than he had been for days.

The swing door opened and Roy Culworth came in. He stood looking around the bar for a few seconds and then he saw Gord. He walked slowly across the floor, taking off his topcoat. Roy always wore a light tan raincoat, even in summer. He was about forty and looked sixty. His eyes were pale blue and slightly bulging and his hands had a steady fine tremble so that after a few drinks he had to hold his glass very tightly, clamping his arm against his chest.

"Hullo, Gord," he said. He dropped his raincoat on a chair.

"How are you, Roy?" asked Gord.

"Just fine, Gord, just fine," said Roy. He turned to the bar. "Dop-'n-dam, please," he said. He liked to make a joke of his drinking. The barman poured him a brandy-and-water and Roy sat down. He looked at Gord's glass.

"Rules, Gord?" he asked. They had a gentleman's agreement never to treat one another. It avoided embarrassment.

"Day off?" asked Gord.

"No," said Roy. "I had a difference of opinion with the management, old man."

"It was a good job," said Gord.

"I've had better. I've had much better. They spoke as though they were doing me a favor. I could have put that business on its feet, Gord. Hell, I've managed a business before, you know."

"I know," said Gord. Roy had come into town a year ago. In those days he had had a new car, new clothes, and an accent acquired at the best private school in South Africa. He had taken a room at the Criterion and spent most of his days in the bar. He claimed to have managed a business in Durban. Some days he claimed to have managed a hotel on the Natal South Coast. He spoke with great authority and said he was in town to scout up business opportunities for a friend in Durban. This friend had money and he and Roy were going to go into business together. One day a man from a Johannesburg finance company arrived and took away Roy's Buick. After that Roy stopped talking about his friend. He spent more and more time in the bar and finally took a job as counter hand in Meikle's Ritz Gent's Outfitters, from which position he had been fired after two weeks, going from there to the Criterion as a barman, from where he was fired for being drunk on duty a week running. Then he had taken a clerical job with De Wet's Sno-Wite Steam Laundry. He had stayed with them a month before, as he told Gord now, mutual antipathy had terminated the relationship, old man.

Gord fetched himself another beer. Roy was on his third brandy. Already his confidence was returning. Roy was convinced he could never lose. Every morning he brushed his double-breasted blazer with the yacht club badge and naval buttons, knotted his old school tie neatly around the collar of his silk shirt, and brushed fluff from his light gray flannels. But now the elbows of the blazer were starting

[77]

to shine and the knees of the flannels were beginning to bag and the collar of the silk shirt was just a little frayed. Looking at Roy, Gord wondered how long Roy would outlive his clothes. He's going slowly, thought Gord. Bit by bit, like a river bank crumbling. He listened to Roy talking without hearing the words and thought, the last thing that will go will be that accent, that Durban, best school accent. Soon Roy will start to fade faster and faster and faster until only the accent will be left, like the Cheshire cat in *Alice in Wonderland,* only that was a grin, not an accent.

"I had one of my attacks and took Monday off," said Roy. He was talking about his last employer, the Sno-Wite Steam Laundry. "I'm not a kaffir. Hell, I'm not a kaffir. I told De Wet junior I wasn't a kaffir. If I'm ill, I'm ill. I had one of my attacks. I can't come to work if I'm having an attack."

His hands were shaking and he was holding his glass hard against the counter to steady it. He had spilled some brandy already and there was a dark stain on his flannels.

"They want to operate," he said. "I went along to the Provincial Hospital and they want to operate. That's all these quacks want to do, open you up. I told them, hell, I'm not having my head opened by anyone but the best. They didn't like that. I can tell you, Gord, they didn't like that at all."

"I don't suppose they did," said Gord. Roy bored him and frightened him. Watching Roy was like watching himself in a mirror. He did not want to end up like Roy. He was nearly twenty years older than Roy but he still didn't want to end up like that.

"A tumor is a dreadful thing," said Roy. He was trying to be brave about it.

"It's a dreadful thing to have hanging over one, but one mustn't let it get one down," he said. "I try not to let it get me down. Other chaps would go to pieces, but I hang on."

"Are they sure about it?" asked Gord. He was being polite. Roy didn't have a tumor. His attacks were delirium tremens. Roy knew it and everybody knew it. In the Provincial Hospital he had been dried out and discharged. He had been in three times since arriving in town. When he was having an attack the trembling of his hands became worse and worse until his arms were jerking wildly, flapping, while his legs twitched and kicked. In the Criterion one night it had taken the manager and the bar boy to hold him on the bed. Gord had gone up to help them. He still remembered the bar boy, a young Xhosa, holding Roy down, shaking his head in sympathy, his eyes very white in his dark face, shaking his head and clucking "*Au*, Baas Roy!" while Baas Roy, jerking and twitching and grunting and exhibiting none of the traditional dignity of the white man, dirtied his pants and the hotel sheets, to the great annoyance of the manager, who gave him notice the next morning.

"I have a tumor of the brain," Roy told people. "It is a tumor which effects the motor-centers of the brain at intervals, causing spasmodic convulsions. It has nothing to do with liquor. I have seen a specialist in Durban." After many years he believed in the tumor himself. It had become an integral and essential facet of his personality. Without it he would have lost all faith in himself. As it was, he still had a little, enough to make him press his trousers and brush his blazer and polish his boots.

"They won't admit it," said Roy. "They won't admit it. They know they can't handle it and they won't admit it."

"I thought you said they wanted to operate," said Gord.

"Well, they didn't actually admit it, but you can see they're wavering. An exploratory operation, that's what they call it. I won't have it. Would you, Gord? Would you have it?"

"I don't know," said Gord. "Guess not. It all depends." The bar was quite full now. It was nearly one. Tom Pithey was drinking in the far corner. He saw Gord and stood up and walked across.

"Morning, Gord," he said. "Hullo, Roy."

He sat down. He was wearing his best suit with a small yellow flower in the buttonhole.

"Going to the lunch?" asked Gord.

"Every Wednesday," said Pithey. "You see Doctor Hammersley?"

"No. Not since last week."

"He's looking for you. Got some shooting he wants done."

"I've seen his kind of shooting," said Gord. "He c'n get someone else. Not me. I've seen him and his friends."

"You can't afford to talk like that, Gord," said Pithey.

"I can afford not to become a bloody butcher," said Gord.

"Let me just tell you about the job," said Pithey.

"I don't want to hear."

"I'm going to tell you, Gord. I'm going to tell you because things are getting tight for you in this town and they're going to get tighter, a bloody sight tighter. Now you listen to me."

Gord shrugged.

"I'm not interested."

"You know that block of land along the reserve? Long strip, about three thousand morgen?"

"Yes. Full of prickly pear, jointed cactus, droog-m'-keel and mimosa."

"Right. It's also full of game. The homestead's stood empty for ten years. Buck've bred like flies. Duiker, kudu, oribi, bushbuck, anything you can think of. Well, the doctor's bought it."

"Good luck to him," said Gord. He was starting to feel the three beers now. "The best of luck to him."

"It's also full of donkeys," said Pithey. He was watching Gord very closely.

"They brought a couple pairs into the district years ago to pull some kaffir carts. They got away into the bush and now there's about forty of them. The doctor reckons they're wild as buck. He wants them shot out. Says they're eating the grazing he wants for buck. He's talking of putting eland in."

"Tom," said Gord. "Go to your lunch. Please go to your lunch before I get very impolite."

"He's paying fifty bob a head, Gord. He wants them shot and slaughtered. He's going to make biltong for his dogs."

"From forty donkeys? Must have a lot of dogs."

[81]

"It's a hundred quid, Gord. You need it. Don't tell me you don't need it."

"My finances have nothing to do with you," said Gord. He could feel a small pulse throbbing in his neck.

"Good money," said Roy. He nodded his head wisely. "Very good money, Gord."

"This is nothing to do with you," said Gord. "You keep out of this, Roy."

"I'll let you have cartridges on the book," said Pithey.

"I don't need your credit," said Gord. "I don't need anything from you at all. Nothing. Now you go to your lunch and tell the doctor what he c'n do with his donkeys."

"It's good business," said Roy. "It's good business, Gord."

"You shut up, Roy," said Gord. "You keep right out of this."

"There's a kaffir in Sonderwater'll do it," said Pithey. "The doctor hasn't heard from you by Friday, he's going over to get the kaffir. We just thought you'd like the chance, that's all."

"Thanks, Tom. Thanks very much. Now you go to lunch." Pithey stood up.

"Remember what I said, Gord. Your credit's not too good in this town any more. People hear you turned down a job paying a hundred quid, it's likely to get a lot worse."

"Meaning with you?"

"Meaning with all of us. I've heard them talking up there, you know." He raised his eyes to indicate the Royal Buffet and Grill Room upstairs.

"Your name's not very good, Gord."

"A donkey-butcher," said Gord. "You think it'll be any better when I'm a donkey-butcher?"

"You want to forget this white hunter stuff, Gord. We're all getting tired of it. You got to earn your money where you can get it now. And right now you can get it on Hammersley's land."

"I don't want to discuss it," said Gord. "I'm tired of the subject."

"He's right, Gord," said Roy. "It's good money."

"Please mind your business, Roy," said Gord. He stood up and put on his hat. His hands were trembling slightly and that annoyed him.

"You'd better think about it," said Pithey.

"I've told you what he can do with his donkeys," said Gord. "And you."

He walked out into the street. There was no wind and the sky was pale blue with thin wind clouds very high. The sun on the white dusty street hurt his eyes. He tilted his hat down over his nose and walked along the pavement. His stomach was fluttering with nervous anger. I should get something to eat, he thought. I must also get Julia's thread. I'll get her thread and then eat. The beers had made him feel heavy and slightly nauseated. I'll go home and sleep, he thought. I'm too old to drink at lunchtime. It makes me sleepy. His bad leg was aching again, not much, but enough to worry him. I hope it's not going wrong, he thought. Not just now. On the corner were three pepper trees and a municipal bench. He sat down and stretched his legs. I'd like to go to sleep now. Just doze off. The pepper trees broke the sunlight and with his eyes closed he could feel the dappled shadows against the lids. Somewhere a dove was calling *ku-kurrr ku-kurrr* and in the gutter across the street a red winged spreeuw was bathing, the big flight feathers very red when it fanned its dark blue wings. He's a smart boy, thought Gord, watching him. The bird had a sleek dark head and bright yellow eyes. His mate, a plump hen with light gray head, sat watching him from the curb. When the cock had finished bathing they flew away over the rooftops in big swoops and arcs.

He dozed a little and then the bench creaked as somebody sat down beside him. He looked up, resentful, and saw that it was Roy.

"May I join you?" he asked.

"It's a public bench," said Gord. He never wanted to be rude to Roy but he was getting terribly bored with him and he thought that if Roy was now going to start interfering in his affairs it was time to break up the friendship, if it could be called that.

"I've annoyed you," said Roy. He was pretty drunk. Gord could smell the brandy. He had always hated smelling drink on people, and out in the open it always seemed worse. I'll bet Roy's whole oufit smells of brandy, he thought. Bet you could wring him out like a sponge and you'd get a bottle of it.

"I've annoyed you," said Roy. "I'm sorry, Gord. Just wanted to say I'm sorry."

"That's all right," said Gord. He wished Roy would go. He closed his eyes again.

" 'F' you want an extra gun on that trip, I'm your man," said Roy. "You c'n count on me, Gord."

Gord opened his eyes. He was both irritated and amused and a little embarrassed. Roy was sitting very straight. His blazer was buttoned and he had straightened his tie and he had what he believed was a bushman's look on his face, lips very compressed, eyes narrowed, and it was very sad because he wasn't trying to be funny at all.

"I held a commission with the Natal Carabineers," he said. "I held the King's Commission. Still got it somewhere. Just a piece of paper, but it meant something then, Gord, it did. Decent regiment. Fine crowd of chaps. Left a lot of them in the desert."

"I thought you were with the SAAF," said Gord. That was nasty, he thought. That was really nasty. But Roy was annoying him again. I don't mind so much when he's just a drunk. I don't mind when he bulls us about his big jobs. But he needles me when he starts this old soldier business. So now he's an ex-infantry officer. Time before he was in the SAAF. Time before that he was with the Long-Range Desert Group. One time he was in the Royal Navy ("Seconded, old boy, against my bloody wishes, I can tell you, to help the Limey commandos at Dieppe. Bloody fine show, but botched from up top, of course.")

"I was washed out of the SAAF" said Roy. He sounded hurt. "Early in the war. Pranged a Spittie outside Mersa Matruh. Bloody silly thing to do. C.O. was furious. Hated my guts. Sent me back to the Union. I wangled a transfer to the Carabineers. Friend of mine at Roberts Heights pulled strings."

Oh please shut up, thought Gord. Please shut up and go

away. I don't like you but I don't want to hurt you. Please just go back to your booze.

"I was pretty good with a three-o-three, Gord," said Roy. "Nothing like the old three-o-three. Wonderful weapon. I was pretty good with it then. Of course, the old peepers aren't what they were, but I'm still pretty good."

"I'm not interested," said Gord. "You were there when Pithey spoke to me, Roy. You heard me tell him nothing doing."

"Well, if you decided to, Gord, if you decide to do it for them, I'm your man, eh, Gord?"

Gord looked at him. He really means it. He really means it. He really wants me to give him a job. Well, my God, that's a change. That's a change all right. Somebody asking me for a job.

"Fact is, old man," said Roy. "Fact is, I'm a bit short this month. My money hasn't come through yet. Blasted red tape. Caught me a bit short. Could use a few quid."

"I'm not doing it, Roy. I told you back in the bar I wasn't doing it."

Gord stood up. He was really very tired of Roy and now he was sorry for him and ashamed of him together. Please God I'm never like this, he thought. Never like this. Never ever like this. He looked at the neat blazer and the yacht club tie and the baggy flannels and the once shiny shoes and felt a sudden contempt. He turned and walked back along the pavement. The drink was heavy in him now and he felt old and tired and his bad leg was throbbing softly and insistently.

"Well, if you need me," said Roy.

[86]

"I won't need you," said Gord.

"I need it, Gord," said Roy, and suddenly he wasn't anything but a beaten shabby man in baggy flannels and a shiny blazer with his fine-threaded cheeks senile in the bright sunlight and his eyes in their dirty-shadowed pits were frightened, more frightened than eyes Gord had ever seen.

"I'll remember you if anything comes up," he said.

"Please, Gord. I'll be all right. Won't let you down."

"I'll remember," said Gord. He turned and walked away, walking very quickly down the hot pavement, crossing the street to walk in the shade of the long overhanging balcony of the divisional council building. It was a wide flat balcony with a low iron railing and in the summer the office staff used it as a terrace. At the corner he stopped and looked back, very briefly. Roy was sitting on the bench watching the traffic.

14

$\mathcal{G}$ORD went on down the street and into Mick's Syrian Café and sat down at a corner table. His hands were trembling and he kept them in his lap while the waitress took his order. He ordered sausages and chips and coffee. He ate without raising his eyes because he did not feel like talking and Mick was a very talkative Syrian. He had come to South Africa just after the war and started this small café. The whole Mick family worked in it. In the town they were always referred to as the Mick family because Mick's last name was quite unpronounceable. Mick was dark and good-looking and played golf to a fifteen. He was a member of the town council and the Rotary Club. He spoke very good English. It was better, in fact, than the English spoken by anyone else in the town. He claimed to have been an interpreter with the French Army Intelligence during the war. His wife was dark, fat, friendly, and quite incomprehensible. In five years in the country she had only picked up a dozen words of English. The ones she used most were *hullo* and *goodbye,* always at the wrong time, and *hey man,* for which she had a surprising range of variations. She and Mick and their two dark plump daughters, as inarticulate as their mother, ran the café with occasional waitresses and a cheerful Zulu cook. The café was long and narrow and gloomy, tucked in between two high buildings. There were eight cheap tables without cloths and the whole room smelled of cooking fat and, in the summer, Flit, because Mrs. Mick hated flies and kept the flit gun beside the cash register. In the hot weather, when there were a great many flies in that part of town (the municipal sewage farm was two blocks away) the smell of Flit overcame the cooking smell.

Today it smelled of cold fat and stewed tea. Gord thought he preferred the Flit. He ate quickly and paid Mrs. Mick at the cash desk while Mick was talking to a customer. He felt elated at dodging him. He walked down the street and bought a spool of blue thread and drove home. He was thinking of Roy and the donkeys as he drove into the shed. He sat there in the dimness and listened to the engine cooling with faint pings and crinkles and thought I'm damned if I'll do it. I'm damned if I'll do it. Let them get somebody else to do their butchering. He got out and closed the shed door and walked up to the house very determined. He still felt drowsy from the beer but he was all right now and the ache in his leg had stopped.

15

$\mathcal{T}$HAT night he cleaned the guns. Every month, whether they had been fired or not, he brought the guns into the kitchen and cleaned them, stripping the actions, pulling through the barrels, oiling the stocks. He thought of them as a plumber thinks of his tools. He liked to look at them lying there on the scrubbed table, the long barrels blue-brown in the lamplight, the stocks smooth and glowing. He liked the smell of machine oil and cordite and the beautiful oily syllables of a good action being cocked. I'm a silly old man, he thought, looking at them now, I'm a silly old man, but I love these things, these long lumps of metal. There was a single-barrel hammer-fired 12-bore by Greener: the stock was cracked and had been bound with copper wire. He had taken it in payment of a debt. The previous owner had cracked the stock hitting a wounded duiker, which Gord thought branded him as a greenhorn in the bush. You never clubbed wounded game, and certainly not with expensive shotguns. But people did stupid things with guns. There was the station commander at Rooihoogte who shot himself with his own Smith & Wesson .38 at a party. He

[90]

took a cartridge out of the chamber under the hammer when nobody was looking, and then announced that as his party trick he would shoot himself. He forgot that when he cocked the revolver a loaded chamber would come up under the hammer. It was his last party trick and it made an awful mess.

Gord had some good guns, guns he had collected over the years. He still liked the old army model Lee-Enfield. There were better rifles for hunting, but the Lee-Enfield was a good, accurate, rifle and probably the cheapest .303 in the world. Everyone used them. It was a heavy gun to carry but he didn't mind that. The clip held nine rounds which was handy; it would take ten, but the extra load strained the magazine spring. It wasn't a good stopping gun, compared with guns like the Mannlicher and the big Mausers, but he had great faith in his ability to put a soft-nose anywhere he wanted to. He looked at the guns on the table and thought that if there was one thing he could do it was shoot. It was the only thing he had managed to do really well. He had missed very few shots in his life. When he was young they had never had much money. He remembered going into the bush after buck with two rounds in the magazine. Good shooting was in those days a matter of economy as well as pride. Well, it was now, he thought. It is now, all right. The only time he had ever had enough ammunition was during the war. Up in Tanganyika they had gone into the bush with two hundred rounds each. But even then the habit of careful shooting had stuck. He had never been the sort of man who blazes away, in war or peace. He shot as carefully at a standing man as he did at a running buck.

He was glad all that was over now. The excitement of war had ended for him when he saw his first dead. They had engaged a strong patrol of African and European soldiers along the Wami River. When Gord came up to the line with the second platoon of askaris they found a section of Africans with a German officer who had been caught in the long grass. They were lying tumbled on either side of the path in the tall yellow grass. They had been retreating down the narrow path when the British patrol caught them. In the narrow path they had got in each other's way. The officer was a fat man in his forties. When Gord found him he was sitting on his wide haunches beside the path, with his legs folded underneath him in an effeminate way, although there was nothing effeminate about his face. A bullet had hit him above the collar and come out under his eye. It had been deflected and flattened by the thickness of the skullbones, and had come out raggedly, scattering most of the officer's face on the grass. Only one eye remained, cold blue and quite disinterested, staring down the path. He had been behind his men when they retreated down the path.

The dry sand was muddy with blood. Most of the African soldiers were lying on their faces. One had his rifle slung over his shoulder. The bodies smelled of old sweat and already the bluebottles were buzzing over the blood. Somewhere further up the path the rifles began firing again, a far-off, flat *pop-pop-pop*. The bush muted the gunfire and made the whole thing sound very civilized, like the desul-

tory shooting on a rifle range on a quiet summer afternoon.
Gay umbrellas and parked cars and tea in the ladies' com-
mittee tent. Only the dead lying untidily in the grass beside
the path spoiled the picture. Gord and his men went up the
path in the hot blood and sweat-smelling afternoon and the
dead German officer watched them with his one eye. He
had a broad webbing belt and on the buckle it said GOTT
MIT UNS. It hadn't been cleaned for a long time but you
could still read the words. In the crevices it was green with
verdigris. The afternoon wind stirred the tops of the tall
grass and the officer's hair fluttered slightly in the breeze
as Gord's men went past him and up to the line.

That finished me, thought Gord. That man. That casual-
ness. No matter what they tell me, no matter how they
explain it, that will never be right. We defile everything.
He died for no cause. Does he need their medals? Do they
even know where he died, how he died? And yet he died
because he was fighting for something he believed he believed in. Do we do what we do because we believe in
what we are doing, or do we believe in it because the poli-
ticians have put us in such a position that we have to believe
in it, to keep our self-respect, our honor, our decency? Oh
God, he thought, oh God, I'm going to have an awful lot
of questions to ask when I get up there. He was not at all
sure that he was going to heaven, but he was quite sure
that some chain of authority existed up there, and he was
equally sure that he was going to question the first being in
authority he met. He wished more deeply than he had ever
wished for anything in his whole life that he had Julia's

faith. That must be a wonderful thing, that faith. It is always right. No matter what is done it is always right.

Along the Rufiji he had murdered a man. There was no other word for it. They were under fire from mountain guns on a high bare ridge. The Krupps were dropping all over the ridge, splintering the stone with high frightening noises. He and a subaltern were lying behind an antheap. The subaltern was just out from England. It was his first action and he was enjoying it immensely. He would grin at Gord and pop up from behind the antheap and snap a few shots with his Webley. He loved it. You would have thought he was in a film. When the Krupps fell close he would snuggle in beside Gord, laughing. He was a very good-looking young man, the kind of Englishman who turn very pink in the sun. Gord remembered lying there with his face against the ground and seeing the angry red sunburn on the back of the subaltern's hands. Then the subaltern lifted his head and a shell took his bottom jaw away. He fell back on his hands and knees and shook his head like a stunned ox. His lower jaw was gone and there was a piece of bone with two teeth attached sticking to his shirt. Now he only had an upper jaw and his face was fixed in a huge idiotic grin. He knelt beside Gord and the blood bubbled from his tattered face onto the hard hot earth. His eyes smiled when Gord drew his revolver.

It was the last shot he had ever fired from that Webley, and the best. The subaltern was buried that day. There was no inquiry. Gord's mother was very upset by it. She prayed for Gord every night and from then on she made special intercessions on his behalf. His father approved but never said so because he did not want to worry his wife, who believed that by condoning Gord's act they would share his guilt. It had never worried Gord. He had liked the subaltern very much indeed, too much to let him go on living the way the Krupps had left him. That was all a long time ago. The subaltern's grave was on the ridge where he had died, among the antheaps and prickly pear and red-hot poker flowers. It's a long way from England, thought Gord. A long way from England. I suppose now in my old age it should worry me. He looked at the Webley lying on the table. It was the army model Webley with a squared barrel and a high front sight. I suppose it should worry me but it doesn't. If it'd been me I'd have wanted it the same way. We never could have done anything for him. He wasn't the sort of man who would have wanted to live like that, anyway. But we could never have got him out alive, wounded like that, back down the hill and to the railhead. It was the first time in many years he had thought about the subaltern and the first time he had ever had any doubts about it.

The other handgun was a Luger. It had once been very rusty and the sanded and oiled metal was still pitted. It had belonged to a ranger called Chris Uys. He and another ranger, Boet Erasmus, were riding the boundary of the Kruger Park just after the war when a cow elephant they were herding back into the reserve attacked them. Erasmus's horse broke its leg in a springhare hole and the cow caught him, dragging him out of the saddle and slamming him against the ground and then kneeling on him. Uys was well clear and could have shot the cow without any trouble but when he heard the noises Erasmus made something broke in him and he threw his Mauser away and ran wildly into the bush. His horse trotted into Punda Maria rest camp that night and the next day they found Uys. He was very calm and reserved and would not speak about the elephant or about Erasmus. They brought him back to camp and everyone was very understanding but that night he went off into the thick bush along the Luvuvhu on foot, leaving his horse and rifle in the camp. They followed his spoor for miles the next day but then it rained heavily and they lost it.

Gord knew his family in Johannesburg. They were very worried at the thought of Chris not getting a Christian burial, so six months later they financed Gord to find him. Gord was recuperating from his leg wound then and pretty bored with Johannesburg, and he and a Zulu worked along the river for days. They picked up the trail in the end and found Chris Uys in a prickly pear thicket. He had walked for twenty miles through the bush before crawling deep into the cactus like a wounded animal and shooting himself with the Luger. The big red ants and the hyenas had not left much of Chris.

They brought him back to Punda Maria in a mealie sack and the next day he was buried in the public cemetery at Nelspruit. Gord and the Zulu were the only mourners. Afterward Gord paid the Zulu and walked through the pretty town, with its bright flame trees and wide streets, and sent a telegram to Chris's people in Johannesburg, telling them that he had been decently buried and asking if he could keep the Luger. He hung around Nelspruit for three days but they never replied so he cleaned up the gun, which was very badly rusted, and then moved on down to Natal.

He finished cleaning the guns and put them away and went to bed. Julia was already asleep and he undressed with the lamp turned down low. The wind had dropped and the night was very quiet. Somewhere in front of the house a bullfrog was croaking. It lived in a damp reedy patch beneath the rainwater tank. Gord had never seen a bullfrog living alone like this before. He wondered how it had ended up under his rainwater tank, miles from any big water, or even any decent-sized dam. It was a big fat green-and-yellow frog and very aggressive. It had a deep harsh croak, a penetrating *gaaark!* which sounded like a question.

16

Just below the old farmhouse there was a shallow dam. It was fringed with tall coarse grass and a flat-leaved plant whose name they never knew. The dam was shallow enough to stand in. It only came up to Gord's armpits when he was fifteen. They used to swim in it in summer. The top layer of water was lukewarm but from two feet below the surface it was very cold, even in summer. Underfoot the bottom was squashy and teeth-edgy with rotting vegetation and the squirmy feel of strange insects. There were big bullfrogs in the grass, and water tortoises living in the dam. Once they had tried to keep duck on the dam but the bull-frogs and the water tortoises had eaten all the ducklings as soon as they were old enough to swim. In the evenings all the birds for miles around came to drink at the dam: turtledoves, bush doves, mousebirds, blue spreeuws, red-wing spreeuws, tickbirds, white and dainty, fat self-confident hadedahs, cautious crows, scuttling wary guinea fowl. In those long quiet evenings the weaver birds had made a steady buzzing in the tall gums behind the dam until after dark. He liked walking back to the farmhouse

*after sunset, with the warmth of the day still in the soil,
the beetles stirring and flying in the long grass, the crickets
piping, the birds muttering and twittering, the lights of the
house warm and yellow against the sky, the smell of the
gumwood smoke coiling down the still air towards him,
drifting down the silent shadowed valley behind him like
low fog. There was a lot of game around the farmhouse
in those days. They shot very little. The pheasants would
come up from the valley and eat with the farm chickens
at the evening and morning feeding times. Hares came
into the yard at night. He often sat at his upstairs window
on moonlight nights and watched them. One big buck hare
always hung around the outside lavatory, one of those
tin shed-and-bucket affairs. Night after night Gord would
see him when he went up to the shed before going to bed.
The hare was very tame and quite used to people and
nobody ever bothered him until one moonlight night a
house guest shot him from the window of the upstairs
bedroom. In the morning when Gord went up to the shed
he was still lying there, his fur sparkling with dew, his
ears big translucent pink fans on the wet grass. He lay
there all day until one of the Africans found him and carried him, head and feet flopping, white stub tail bouncing,
to the slaughter shed. Nobody said anything to the guest
but he left after breakfast.*

17

THE weather was hotter. Alongside the road the grass
was dry and dusty and the hills were more brown than
green. The nights and mornings were still cold but an hour
after sunrise it was hot. Down in the town it was worse.
The air was stale and humid and unpleasant to breathe and
the sewage farm smelled. It was a bad year for flies and the
whole town crawled with them. Every room was steeped
in the smell of Flit and the sticky flypapers, glistening
with trapped bluebottles, oscillating with faint buzzings
from every ceiling.

Gord drove right around the valley during the next few
days and knew it was going to be a bad year. It seemed
that all at once every farmer's son had grown up and decided to bring his friends back for the vacation. The baboons were staying in the hills and the jackal were hiding
deep in the kloofs and the dassies which had always been
Gord's last resort were so sniped at by the holiday hunters
that they stayed in their holes for most of the day. In a
week he shot one stray baboon and two dassies and at the
end of it he knew there was not much farther to go. He

hadn't made enough to pay for his gasoline and it would be two weeks before the kids had gone back to their schools and agricultural colleges and universities, and at least a week after that before the bush was any good for him. He was confused and worried by the suddenness of everything. This had been coming for a long time but now it had happened all at once; all of a sudden everyone's kids were grown up and the farms were wanted for them and their friends, not for him, a limping anachronism (although he didn't know the word), a man from another time.

One day he drove up to Hammersley's piece of land. It was a long strip bordering the reserve. The land fell away towards the river in a broad sweep of prickly pear and droog-m'-keel and mimosa. Most of it was prickly pear, though. Gord had never seen it so thick. The thick gray green leaves formed solid walls of vegetation. Some of the leaves were wilted and patchy with the cotton wool cocoons of the cochineal insect, which had been introduced some years before to kill off the cactus, but most of the plants were thick-leaved and healthy. The strip was fenced with six strands of barbed wire, strung from steel railway ties. He drove slowly along the boundary road. It was very quiet and only a faint wind stirred the bush. In the pear he could hear guinea fowl and pheasants and twice he saw duiker, a solitary ewe and then a ram and two ewes. The bush beyond the barbed wire looked thick and unspoiled and he thought he would like to take a walk through it. Once you were among the pears and mimosa you wouldn't be able to see the fence or the road or any windmills or telegraph lines. He drove slowly along the bad road, all potholed and overgrown, and suddenly, after keeping his eyes on the road for a particularly bad stretch, he looked up and saw the donkeys strung out on a low rise just beyond the fence, interested but not yet frightened. He stopped the car and they began to trot over the hill, not panicked, but taking no chances. They were all in good shape, lean and glossy, not swaybacked and shaggy like town donkeys. There was a big jack leading them, almost black, with fine stiff ears and the cross on his shoulders very pronounced. The big jack stopped on the top of the slope and the others went past him, a few smaller jacks and a dozen jennies and a few knobby-kneed foals. When they were all over the big jack flicked his tail and trotted after them, over the hill and into the bush. Gord started the car and drove on to the end of the road and then drove back, slowly, looking at the land behind the barbed wire and thinking how he would do it, because he knew now that he was going to do it, and if he did it he wanted to do it properly. He still did not want to do it but he was a realist and he knew he had to. Looking at the donkeys had not made any difference. He had never been an indiscriminate hunter, but he had never been a sentimentalist, either. He didn't want to shoot the donkeys. He didn't want to have anything to do with it. But it was going to be done in any case and he might as well do it, both for the donkeys and himself.

He turned onto the national road and drove home. The knock in the engine was a steady rattle now. He listened to it and thought that he should feel happier now that his mind was made up but he didn't. It grew dark before he got home. He drove very carefully because he was finding it harder to drive at night.

When he was over the hill behind his house he switched the engine off and rolled down the hill, turning sharply, at his gate skidding a little, and coasting right into the shed. It was one of his little economies.

After supper he told Julia about the donkeys. He spoke for a long time. He reminded her of their debts, of the knock in the Ford's engine, or the leaking roof over the kitchen. He explained that he didn't want to do it but he had to do it, that he thought Hammersley was a fool and his friends butchers. He told her that if he didn't do it they would undoubtedly get some kaffir who would poison them or trap them or hunt them with a pack of kaffir dogs. She listened without interrupting, her face as serene and unworrried as before. When he was finished he felt exhausted, drained, and a little ashamed of himself.

"'Well?" he said, when he had finished. "Well, Julia?" He was defensive.

"Gord, you do it. But you don't have to do it. If you want to, do it."

"I have to. You know that."

"You don't have to do anything at all, Gord. Not anything at all."

"You talk like that. Have you heard the Ford? You know what a job like that costs?"

"You could do it yourself. You used to do everything like that yourself."

"I had a block-and-tackle then. And tools. And I had friends to help me."

"You can borrow tools."

"Not in this town I can't. I wouldn't ask them for anything at all in this town."

"Gord, I don't want you to do anything you don't like. It's just not worth it."

"It's worth a hundred quid," he said. He was very bitter because he knew she was right. It wasn't worth it. It wasn't worth it at all but he was going to do it.

"It's not worth any money at all to me to see you unhappy," she said, looking at him. "You know that, Gord. I've never worried about money and you know that's true."

"I wish I had your confidence," he said.

"It's not confidence. It's happiness. It's serenity." She lifted her hand as though to show him something and then he saw she was holding a Bible in her lap.

"I don't have it," he said. "I don't have it. I've never had it and I can't have it now."

"I wish you'd come to church with me," she said.

"We argued that out ten years ago," he said. He was beginning to feel angry.

"I know," she said. "But I wish you had faith. You have no faith, no resignation."

"I have no faith," he said. "I simply cannot have faith. I cannot have faith or resignation."

"I'll make some more coffee," she said. He watched her while she worked over the stove, filling the kettle, spooning coffee into the pot, pouring in the boiling water. The coffee smelled rich and good. She poured two cups, added milk and sugar, and brought them to the table. He sat looking at her while she drank. The firelight was kind to her. Her face was at rest and completely unworried and she looked twenty years younger. He felt quick irritation at her smugness and then realized that it wasn't smugness at all. In that moment he envied her terribly.

Once he had finally made up his mind that he was going to do it he felt better. It was as though the responsibility had been taken from him, as though a chain reaction had been set up which he was unable to stop. After coffee he checked the Lee-Enfield and the twelve-bore. He would use the .303 and Roy could backstop him with the shotgun. He would take Roy along. He needed somebody else and there was nobody else he could ask. He had no faith in Roy at all, but he needed another man. And there was that old Swazi Elias working in the Royal. He had been a game ranger in the Hluhluwe rhino reserve before a crocodile had taken his leg somewhere along the Pongola. Elias could do the skinning. He didn't need two legs for that. My God, thought Gord, we're a fine bloody trio. A nearly senile old man, a drunkard, and a crippled kaffir.

18

After work he liked walking through the park. His knee was still stiff and he used a stick sometimes. He liked the long summer evenings and the sudden sharp Transvaal thunderstorms. The park had tall blue-gum trees and old pines that the wind sighed in even on still days. Underneath the pines the fallen brown needles were slippery and he had to walk carefully. There were beds of bright red-and-yellow cannas along the gravel paths and roses on the lawns. Johannesburg was having a very dry summer and water restrictions were in force but the mine had its own water and so the hoses and automatic sprinklers trickled all day and a small army of gardeners, mine pensioners and war cripples weeded, raked, mowed and pruned all day. The park was on a hill above the town and the traffic noises filtered through the trees as far off and distant as the mutter of far away surf after a storm.

The park was full of birds. Migratory stork nested in the pines, and egrets with them, and there were always blue cranes stalking the lawns. The lower end of the park had been leveled and graveled, and behind a screen of orange-flowering gum, two tennis courts and a split-pole pavilion had been built. The mine had a very active recreation club and in the summer evenings the courts were always crowded with young men and women in white. Gord liked watching them. He had never played tennis but he wanted to try when his knee was stronger. He liked the tennis courts. He liked the smell of gravel and lime mingled with the smell of the flowering gums and shoe whiting and he liked the young people who played so happily and unconcernedly. He wasn't much older than most of the young mine employees but he felt of a different generation. But these people in this context did not offend him. He was, after all, a temporary guest in their world, until his leg healed. So they neither bothered nor irritated him, nor did they make him envious. He sat on the low split-pole bench and drank raspberry syrup from the old colored woman's concession stall and watched the darting, laughing figures and felt neither the fierce resentment nor the bitter envy which was to poison his life later, when their world overtook his.

One Tuesday evening he went down to the courts after work and there was only one player there, a young girl he had not seen before. She was sitting on the bench in the pavilion. She had short dark hair and a wide mouth in a very tanned, thin face. She was bouncing her racket against her foot and looking irritable when Gord stretched out on his bench. Gord guessed she had arranged to meet the others there and they had let her down, probably because it looked like it was going to rain. There had been the feeling of thunder in the air all day and sheet lightning was flickering in the north and clouds were banking over the town. Gord sat and watched her. After a while she stood up and walked across the court to him, swinging her racket. He stood up.

"Good evening," she said. "Have you been here long — I mean, did you see anyone who looked as though they might have been waiting for me?"

"No," he said. "I come down most nights. Usually the crowd's here, but I haven't seen 'em tonight. Guess they're frightened it'll rain."

"I took a chance," she said. "They said don't come if it looks like rain, but it hadn't rained when I left the house."

"It'll rain. Been banking up to it all day. It'll come down in buckets, all right."

"I didn't think it would frighten them off," she said. "Sugar babies."

"You can't play on a wet court. Plows up the gravel."

"I know," she said. "But it hasn't rained yet, has it?"

Thunder rumbled in the hills behind the town and there was a brief flicker of lightning in the clouds.

"No," he said, smiling, and wondering how he could keep her talking, "not yet."

"We could have a knock until it comes down," she said. "Do you play?"

"Never tried," he said. He stood up and flexed his knee, testing it.

"Oh. Your leg," she said. "I'm sorry."

"It's mending," he said. "I'll give it a try. Do it good, most probably. What do the quacks call it? — therapy?"

"If you think you should," she said. "You can stand in

*one spot and I'll serve to you. I'll put them right next to
you so you won't have to run. Will that be all right? What
did you do to your leg? Break it?"*

"Somebody shot me," he said.

"You mean in the war?"

*"No. Up in Mozambique. It was an accident. He was
drunk. It's a few months ago now. Leg's still pretty stiff.
It was a big bullet and it smashed the knee cap and the
two leg bones — the tib- something or other and the other
one."*

*"The tibia and fibula," she said, smiling. "Oh, I'm not
that clever, but I am a nurse. That must have been terrible.
You're lucky you didn't lose your leg. But do you really
think you should play?"*

*They walked back to the pavilion and she picked the
lock on one of the lockers and gave him somebody's racket
and they went out on to the court. She lobbed the first few
balls over very slowly and he sent them all back. He got
the knack of it very quickly and she was an accurate server,
putting the balls right beside him, to the right and the left,
so that he never had to take more than a step to reach
them, and then she speeded up, slamming them down hard
and low, skimming the net. She had a very powerful service
for a girl and the balls whistled as they came through. It
was the first real exercise he had had for months and he
sweated a bit but he was still pretty fit and it didn't bother
him at all. He was sorry when the first big drops of rain
pocked the court.*

*"Put the racket under your shirt," she said as they ran
back to the pavilion. "Rain makes the strings soggy."*

[109]

In the pavilion the rain was a steady rattle on the corrugated iron roof.

"I love the smell of the earth when it's raining," she said. "Breathe it in. Isn't it lovely? So fresh."

The rain was falling steadily, straight down, and small pools were forming on the court. A trickle of water ran across the earth floor of the pavilion and the girl pulled her legs up onto the bench.

"Sit down," she said. "Sit down and tell me about your poor leg. Was it a gunfight? Did you shoot him back?"

"It was an accident. He was fooling around with a gun and I went to take it from him and it went off."

He took the bullet out of his pocket and tossed it to her. From rubbing against the cloth in his pocket the lead had become quite shiny. She looked at it with interest.

"It's terribly dented," she said. "You wouldn't think your leg did that."

She sat turning it over in her hand, without any coyness or shudders of revulsion or simulated shock or indeed any of the ladylike reactions he had expected.

"What was it like in the hospital there, in Lourenço Marques? Were they good to you? Is it true they don't give you chloroform?"

He laughed then. She was suddenly very serious.

"They were very good to me, and they certainly did use chloroform."

"You hear such terrible things," she said. "It just goes to show, doesn't it, that you should never believe anything you hear."

He told her about the afternoon at Maricio's. He had

*thought about it a lot and now he could almost laugh about
it.*

"*How exciting,*" *she said, when he had finished. "Just like
the Wild West.*"

"*No,*" *he said, very firmly. "Not like the Wild West at
all.*"

"*No?*" *she said, looking at him. "No. I suppose it wasn't.*"

*He took the bullet from her and put it in his pocket.
He didn't want to talk about it any more.*

"*I've offended you,*" *she said. "You're annoyed, aren't
you?*"

"*No. But does it matter, anyway?*"

"*Now you're being resigned. I hate people who are resigned.*"

"*All right,*" *he said. "I don't want to talk about it any
more, that's all. I don't want to talk about it but I'm not
annoyed and I'm not resigned. Is that all right?*"

"*Now you are being rude. Rude and difficult. I liked you
better when you were resigned.*"

"*My rough bush manners,*" *he said.*

"*Prickly as a porcupine. I don't want to fight you. I hate
fighting people,*" *she said.*

"*We've stopped fighting now. I'll declare an armistice,*"
said Gord.

"*Tell me about yourself,*" *she said. "Tell me what you do
and what you've done and where you were in the war —*"
*She stopped quickly, afraid that she had opened an awk-
ward subject. "I'm sorry. That's nothing to do with me.
Don't mention the war.*"

"It doesn't matter," he said. "I was in it. I was right in it, all right."

"On a front?"

"A sort of front. In Tanganyika. I saw action, if that's what you mean."

"I'm glad. It's not that I despise men who didn't join up. I mean I wouldn't send them white feathers or anything like that; perhaps they had very good reasons for not joining up, but you just don't feel the same about them. I know that it's wrong and that a man has a right to be a pacifist if he wants to, but you never feel the same about them."

"I know," he said. He thought of his brother still in the mud at Passchendaele. You never feel the same about them either way.

The rain had stopped and it was quite dark. Through the trees they could see the sun low down behind streaky clouds. The trees were very black against the thin strip of sunset sky. It was very quiet after the rain. Somewhere in the trees a dove was cooing tentatively. The night wind was moving the branches and it was colder after the rain.

The wind came up stronger as they walked back through the park, the branches throwing down little hard sharp flurries of water as the wind shook them. He took her down to the mine staff quarters and saw her into the nurses' home. The next day he met her for lunch and that night he took her to a very bad cinema show (in South Africa they called them bioscopes then, and still do: it is only by the more sophisticated people that they are called the movies, or the flicks) and after that to coffee in one of those dreadful, cheap South African cafes, smelling of fat and floor polish; bad weak coffee with boiled milk skinning the top. The next day she asked him to join their tennis party. He borrowed money and bought a pair of tennis shoes and white flannels and played a few sets with her friends during the next two weeks. They had nothing in common with him, or he with them, but he tolerated them because of her, and they tolerated him because of her, so perhaps they did have something in common, after all. Her name was Edith Campher and she came from — so her friends told him — a very good Cape family. She had taken her nursing diploma at Rondebosch and then come up north to get away from her family. His association with her opened a window on another world. He was not sure that he liked it. They had their own private principles, their own ambitions, their own private jokes, and he knew that he would never be truly comfortable in that world. It was a visit into a strange country, a country whose language he knew he would never learn. But she moved him so much that he never thought of anything else and after a month he proposed to her and she accepted. He had changed his job by this time. He was working for a motor repair shop in Johannesburg now; the pay was good and he was sure they could live on it. He worked a nine-hour day and at night he took classes in mechanical engineering at the local technical school. He had always been good with his hands and so the work came easily to him, and now he was surprised to find that theoretical knowledge came easily too.

He had three nights a week off and he spent them with

*Edith. They were still so much in love that they didn't
have to say much to each other. He was happy to sit back
and hear her talk. She was a clever girl in a slick way and,
for that time, quite startlingly outspoken. He loved it and
sank into an almost obsessive adulation of her. After three
months of her company the memory of the bush, of Mozambique and Tanganyika, of flamingoes against the dawn
sky, wind in the high hills, smell of a fired cartridge, eye-
smarting tang of wood smoke, long* showwww! *crack of
a wagon whip in a deep valley, all these things faded and
Gord, shaved, clean-shirted, new-shoed, became a townsman, carrying his little packet of sandwiches to work each
day. He liked it, at first. They were saving to get married
and all their talk was of their future together. Sometimes
a treacherous tendril of doubt would uncoil in his mind,
and he would feel guilty: but this only happened when they
were apart. As soon as he saw her again the doubt retreated somewhere far back in his head: but he always
knew it was there.*

*For six months he shut his eyes and his mind to every-
thing but Edith, his job, night classes, the town: he was
quite determined to make it.*

*"What would you end up as, darling?" Edith had asked
him. "A tramp, that's all. A poor white. It's lucky you met
me. I'll make something of you, just you wait and see."*

*And she worked hard on him. He had always spoken
well, and with very good English, so that was no problem.
And, thanks to his father, his manners could pass anywhere. His father's manners had been learned at the Sand-
hurst officers' mess, and he had drilled them into his sons.*

But in other things he fell far below Edith's standards. She made him read the latest books (she cheated herself, claiming to be terribly well-read when in fact she seldom read more than the reviews in the book pages of the Sunday newspaper) and take an interest in what she called "world affairs" and profess an interest in painting which he did not feel. His clothes, too, pained her: gradually she dressed him the way she wanted, in gray flannels, Panama hat, blazer and cravat. She did it all very tactfully, though, so that in the end he felt that he was changing because he wanted to change, and that the whole metamorphosis was quite voluntary.

But she never really succeeded with him socially, so far as changing his friends went. He still liked his old friends, and tolerated hers, and this angered her. He still liked drinking in the cheap bars around the mine, instead of dressing up and going to the fashionable cocktail lounges which were opening in Johannesburg. He still preferred what she called his "rough friends" to her ambitious, going-places, "cultured" acquaintances.

It wasn't that he felt out of place or inferior or even plain uncomfortable with her friends. It was just the opposite. With the assurance of the real bush-man Gord was completely at ease with them, to the extent of appearing condescending. This irritated her. She could never understand his attitude. The fact that he regarded friends as friends, and not as steps up the social ladder, appalled her. But he was in love with her, and she with him. The physical attraction between them was so overpowering that it made them uncomfortable when they were alone together. They had decided, with the idealism of youth in that decade and in that country, not to do anything about it until they were married. They both felt very noble about this and they used to joke about it. It was a shared discomfort and probably the only reason the thing lasted as long as it did.

Gord found that he was drinking more. He could not afford it but that did not stop him. He had never been much of a drinker before, not when he was in Tanganyika or Mozambique, and it annoyed him to become one now. He met Edith most evenings after work, when she was off duty, for drinks on the stoep of the Railway Hotel. It was an old hotel with a curved green balcony roof and fancy fretted woodwork and potted plants in red pots on the stoep. It backed on to the railway station and on windy days the stoep smelled of steam and coal dust and when a train was blowing off you had to shout across the small wicker tables. He did not like the hotel very much himself, but he used it because he felt that in some way it was a measure of the freedom he still had.

He was not exactly unhappy about the way things were going and yet he was not entirely happy either. He was like a buck which gets a whiff of something on the wind, something which goes before it can be recognized, but which disturbs by its very intangibility. When he was a small boy a Cape cart used to pick up the children from three or four of the farms and take them to a small school in the trading store at the crossroads five miles away. The cart had a lot of ground to cover and the driver would not wait. If the girls and boys were not at the pickup point on time he would go on. Gord remembered how slowly he would walk on mornings when he did not feel like school, dragging his schoolbag behind him in the dust, diverting to look at a new molehill, a bird's nest, a locust which a butcher bird had impaled on a mimosa thorn, hoping all the while that the cart would come early and go without him. The cart never did go without him, but each morning Gord left home with the hope that fate would intervene, that the cart would be early, or that something would happen to delay him quite legally — a cow caught in a sloot, or a sheep trapped in a fence, or something. Nothing ever did happen. Now he was honest enough to realize that he was in the same situation, moving irrevocably towards a climax which he was not sure he wanted, and yet, as he had been many years ago, afraid to overtly break the chain. Now, though, he could prod fate a little: he recognized his clinging to his friends, his dislike for her friends, his fondness for the Railway Hotel, his drinking, for what they were, small, sly diversions, reconnoitering the strength of their decision. It was a strange and worrying time for him but they continued to move steadily towards each other.

And then, one frosty winter morning in July, she told him it was finished. They sometimes met at a coffee shop before work. This morning she had just come off night duty. She was still in her white uniform and starched cap and cape. The sun was low over the housetops, bright but without warmth, and the air was sharp and cold and in the street it was windy. They went into the coffee shop and sat down at a table near the window. The table was covered with frayed oilcloth with a pattern of twining red *roses. It was warm in the shop and the windows were steamed over. Edith rubbed her finger over the glass and made a little window in the moisture so they could see the street with the buses passing and the people going to work.*

"Why?" he said. He had felt huge relief at first but now there was something heavy in his stomach and his hands were shaking a little.

"It's just no good," she said. "I've been thinking about it all night, every night, every day, for a long time and it's just no good at all." She was looking out through the clear place in the window.

"You don't mean it," he said. "Something's just upset you. You don't mean this."

"Do you know how long it is?" she asked. "I mean marriage. How long it is? It's too big for me. It's too big a thing for me. I'm not in love with anyone else or anything like that. It's just that I can't go on with it."

"You were keen enough," he said. He was angry now and also beginning to feel the hurt. He sat very quietly for a minute, hoping that the hurt would go away. It was like the belief that a wound does not hurt until you look at it. But this one did. It came right in and closed itself around his bowels until he thought he was going to be sick.

"You were keen enough," he said again. "You wanted it."

"I don't any more. I've changed my mind. I've just changed my mind. You're a man. Can't you see that?"

"Don't you love me?" he asked. His voice was starting to break.

"No."

"You mean just like that?"

"Is there another way to say it? I don't love you. I've just stopped loving you. I've thought about it and thought about it but I get the same answer."

"I'll marry you any time you like," he said. "I know all this waiting has got on your nerves. It doesn't matter if we can't afford it. We can get married as soon as you like."

She shook her head. He saw that she was not even badly upset. She just wanted an end to it.

"I'm just not in love any more," she said. "Can't you understand that, Gord? Not with you, or anybody."

"Anybody?" he said.

"Don't sneer. You don't have to sneer. I made a mistake and I'm sorry."

"It's too sudden. It just doesn't happen like that, not so suddenly."

"That's how it has happened, Gord."

"This time next week you'll be telling somebody else you love them, won't you?" He was hurting badly now and holding on to himself with an effort and he wanted to hurt her, although he knew that his chance to hurt her had gone long ago.

"I don't know. I don't know anything any more. I'm not sure about anything."

"That's a change," he said. "That's really a change." All along he had half-hoped this would happen and now that it was happening he refused to accept it.

"We're not getting anywhere, Gord," she said. She stood

up and hitched her cape around her shoulders and pushed her chair up to the table.

"Goodbye, Gord. Thank you for the coffee."

She went out of the café, closing the door behind her. He saw the scarlet of her cape flash past the clear place in the window and then she was gone. His coffee had cooled and the boiled milk had skinned on the top, and suddenly he remembered the first time he had taken her out. He paid the bill and walked to work through the cold bright windy streets.

That Friday he resigned. He tried to see her all the next week but somehow she was never in when he telephoned and the next weekend he caught the overnight train to Durban. He telephoned her from Durban; this time she took the call, but it was no good at all and it was a relief to both of them when the three minutes were up. The next day he found a job in a garage. He found a cheap room within walking distance of the garage and there were a few cheap cafés around where he could eat but he knew that he was not going to like the town. He spent a month there without even unpacking his suitcase, just taking things from it as he wanted them. Twice he got very drunk and telephoned Edith and after each call he would sober up and hate himself and her. He stopped going to night classes and took to passing his evenings in a bar near his room. It got so that he forgot what it was like to wake up without a hangover. One morning a month after he had left Johannesburg he awoke very early with the sky just turning blue outside his window. The birds were calling in the trees outside the window and he heard

*the first trams rumbling down West Street. It had rained
during the night and water was trickling down the rain-
pipe and splashing into the drain in the courtyard. His
head was surprisingly clear. He lay there for a long while,
listening to the birds and watching the sky get lighter
and hearing the milk boys and the newspaper boys coming
down the street. He knew quite suddenly that he was
standing on the top of the hill and he didn't want to start
going down the other side just then. He got up and
packed very quickly and quietly, his canvas kitbag and
his cardboard suitcase, pushing his clothes in anyhow, and
when he had finished he made himself a cup of coffee,
boiling the water in the enamel coffee pot on the gas ring.
He drank two cups of coffee and then washed out the pot
and cup in the handbasin and packed them in his kitbag
and picked up the bag and case and went quietly out of
the boardinghouse, along the varnish-smelling creaking
corridors, down the steep dark stairs, unhooking the safety
chain on the front door, and out into the early morning
streets. The sun was just over the tops of the houses, and
there was a small fresh wind from the bay, riffling the
jacaranda trees. He walked to the station but there was
not a train out until the afternoon. Outside the station the
rickshas were waiting. The ricksha boys watched him without interest. They could see he was no use to them. They
were big Zulus with elaborate headdresses of horsehair
and feathers and ox-horns. He walked past them and across
the road to the tram stop and caught an early clanking
tram to the outskirts of town. He walked along the road
for a mile and then a farmer came past with his wife and*

two children in a Model A Ford with the body cut away behind the front seat and a flat wooden platform body added. There was a bundle of cane and some bunches of green bananas and two small African picannins on the platform. The farmer drove past Gord and then stopped and reversed weavingly down the dusty road, the Ford's engine whining in the low gear. He leaned out of the window.

"We're going through to Harding," he said. "That any good to you?"

His eyes were tired and behind him his fat wife and the two little boys looked tired and dusty and irritable. Gord guessed they had been driving all night.

"That's fine," said Gord. "Just fine."

"Well, if you don't mind sitting behind with the kaffirs," said the farmer. He was impatient to get on. Sleep crept up on him when he stopped driving.

Gord swung himself up on the platform and the farmer smiled at him over the back of the front seat and put the Ford in gear and they bumped on down the road. Gord settled himself with his back to the wind. The picannins were wrapped in their blankets and he could only see the tops of their heads and their eyes watching him, serious and unsmiling. The Ford bounced and rattled along the rutted road and despite the sun it was cold on the back. They drove through wide canefields, the wind making long sweeping waves on the tall cane thick and green on the low rolling hills, mile after mile after mile of swaying thick cane. They never saw any people in all those miles of cane, but then it was very early in the morning. At noon

they stopped and the farmer's wife made tea and they ate
sandwiches and some of the green bananas and then they
drove on again. The wooden platform was very hard and
the Ford bounced so much on the bad roads that Gord
was frightened he would fall off. He wedged himself
against the back of the farmer's seat and put his arms
around his knees and tried to sleep in the sun. Later in
the afternoon they started climbing up low hills, the Ford
laboring a little with the steepness of the hill and the load,
the four big cylinders hissing and clattering and the trans-
mission whining and then the radiator began boiling and
they had to stop and wait for it to cool and then go back
down the hill to a little stream which crossed the road and
fill the radiator, carrying the water in the teapot because
the farmer had no water bag. When they started off again
the picannins peeled some prickly pears they had picked
while the car was stopped and gave Gord two. They were
almost too ripe and very sweet and juicy, full of small
pips. He ate them very carefully, frightened that there
were still some thorns on them. He tried to speak to the
picannins in Xhosa and Afrikaans and English but it
seemed they only spoke Zulu. They smiled shyly and then
curled up in their blankets again and lay down on the
bouncing platform, wedged up against each other. They
were in no hurry for the Ford to get anywhere.

They got into Harding very late and he booked in at a
small hotel and the next day hitched a lift to Flagstaff and
the day after that to East London and from there he caught
a train through to Port Elizabeth. He found a job there
and made some friends and after a few months he could

think of Edith without it being badly painful any more. The pain had gradually died until only hate remained. He was very sorry about that. He knew that hate was a wasting and consuming emotion and he tried very hard not to hate Edith but she had really hurt him badly and the hate stayed. It stayed for years and years and he never loved another woman that way again, certainly not Julia, not that particular way.

He knew that he was being unjust to Edith, hating her like that, for so many years, and he knew it was bad for him, too. But he hated her very consistently for many years and then he was up in Bloemfontein at the beginning of the 1939 war with some trucks they were delivering from the Ford plant in Port Elizabeth to the army camp at Tempe and he saw her again. It was a quiet Orange Free State Sunday with all the bars and the bioscopes closed and he was sitting in the square with its dusty green trees when she came along the pavement with a tall fair boy of about eighteen whom Gord guessed must be her son.

It was twenty years since he had seen her but he knew her at once. Her face was almost the same except that the years had eroded it, taking the flesh and leaving the bones, so that it reminded him of a sculpture in which the artist had overstressed all the lines and planes and bone shapes and long thin muscles and stringy tendons and curly veins. She walked down the street with the tall boy and Gord sat on the green bench and watched her; and when he saw how she looked now, how steamed out and sun-dried and finished and worn, not in a rough way, but just a used way, just generally and unfeelingly and uncaringly used, with resignation on her face, in the turn of her lips and in her eyes, he felt sorry for her, and strangely ashamed of himself.

He was glad she did not recognize him. She and the boy walked past; and when they had gone up the deserted paper-blown street, he sat and thought about it and found that he felt no satisfaction at all, not as he had thought he would feel it, twenty years after, with the sting gone and only the desire to hurt remaining. But now he felt nothing at all except pity and a little guilt, and maybe regret for the wasted years.

So he came back to Port Elizabeth, to the sea chopped by the southeaster, even the interminable Port Jackson willows green after the Free State, the searchlights staring out to sea along the beachfront, wide-snouted Bofors peering over sandbag walls, the first pilots from Driftsands air school already in their graves between the cypresses in the South End Cemetery.

He had not been to church for years, but he went into St. Mary's on his first night back, slipping shyly into the last pew, and knelt on the cool tiles, saying very quickly and with some embarrassment, I know I wanted her to suffer but I didn't really want it that way, so if it can stop now, even though it's very late, well, I'll do my best in future. Then he said the Lord's Prayer, which was the only prayer he could remember, and left, feeling that he had somehow shifted the responsibility. He knew this was not a very noble attitude, but he tried to be an honest man, especially with himself.

19

$\mathcal{T}$HEY stood in the long dry grass along the boundary fence and watched the stars go out. The night wind was gone and it was very still. It was cool here on the ridge in the morning but later in the day it would get hot. The birds were starting to awake and down in the dry river bed a pheasant was calling. Over the hills to the east the sky was yellow but the valley below them was dark-shadowed. Gord leaned against the fence pole and smoked a cigarette. He listened to the sounds of the awakening bush and felt very unhappy. He wished it were different. He wished he were here for a different reason. He looked at Roy and the Swazi Elias and wished he had not brought Roy. Perhaps he and the Swazi could do it alone. That was a good boy. He was old, nearly Gord's age, but he was a man who stood like a man and walked like a man and talked like a man. Now he stood beside Gord with the lightening sky behind him, standing easily and relaxed with his hands folded across the muzzles of the gun Gord had lent him. He was wearing patched khaki trousers and a railwayman's cast-off black shirt and an old sport coat.

His head was bare and the small tight curls were turning gray. He stood silently beside Gord listening to the bush. There's not many kaffirs I'd trust with a gun, thought Gord, but this is one of them. Perhaps this is the only one of them. I wish I'd come with him alone. I'd feel better then, maybe, although I don't think anything would make me feel better.

"Time soon, Bass Gord," said Elias. It was quite bright over the hills now and on the mountaintops across the valley the first sun was falling yellow on the grass.

Roy got out of the car and came across the grass towards them. He had had a bad night and Gord could smell the old liquor on him.

"Ready?" he asked. He was carrying the shotgun.

"Be careful with that," said Gord. "Don't poke the barrel in the ground or you'll blow your head off."

"I'm all right, Gord," said Roy. "I'm all right."

"I hope so," said Gord.

"You haven't got a spot of anything, have you? I could do with a little *regmaaker*, Gord. It'd pull me right."

"Nothing'll pull you right," said Gord. "Not now." It was much lighter now and the sun was on Roy's face and he looked worse than Gord had ever seen him look before. Every time I see him he looks worse than the time before, thought Gord. He took a handful of buckshot shells from his pocket and gave them to Roy. Roy put them in his coat pocket. His hands were trembling a little. He broke the shotgun and slid two shells into the chambers.

"Left barrel's choke," said Gord. "Right's open. Don't shoot at all over fifty yards. Use the choke all the time, unless you have to shoot again in a hurry. Hold the gun tight in. She kicks like a mule. Remember, don't use the open barrel. Shot spreads too much."

"I know, Gord," said Roy. He sounded hurt.

"All right," said Gord. "Now shut up."

They walked along and down the ridge, the grass scraping against their trousers. They skirted the dry riverbed and came up the other side of the valley. Gord had come out with Elias the day before and they had found a narrow donga off the main valley with prickly pear growing thick down the sides, making a natural wall. They had blocked off the end of the donga with mimosa thorn, building a high thick barricade. They were going to chase the donkeys down from the wide end of the valley and turn them at the fence. They would try to escape up the donga but the mimosa would stop them and behind them would be three men with guns. Or two and a half men, thought Gord, angrily. Two and a half men, and one of them a kaffir. It's not going to be nice. It's not going to be nice at all. They walked without speaking. Down in the valley it was colder and the dew was still heavy. They put up a hare in the long grass and he loped away slowly, quite unfrightened by the men. The birds were out now and the sun was up. Three duck passed overhead, flying over the hill, their wings making a dry whirring. A duiker jumped up and clattered away, sliding on the loose river gravel in his panic. Then they were out of the bush again and on the open slope, dotted with mimosa and droog-m'-keel bush, and across an open space the donkeys were moving uneasily, just awake and nervous. As the men came out of the shadowed bush the donkeys went quietly down into the valley, moving quietly at a trot, jerking their heads and looking back, not really frightened yet, but taking no chances.

"We'll let them take their time," said Gord. He stopped and leaned the Lee-Enfield against an antheap and lit a cigarette.

"They'll take the easy way down the valley. We'll give them a chance to get down there."

He gave the Swazi a cigarette and they squatted down beside the antheap. He looked around for Roy but he was sitting down ten yards back along the path.

"Roy," said Gord, softly.

"Coming," said Roy. Gord looked at Elias. The Swazi was smiling. He made the motion of lifting a glass to his lips, looking back at Roy.

"He got a half-jack there, Baas Gord. That baas, he brought a half-jack with him. I see it in the car."

Gord felt the anger coming up in, white hot and painful so that he felt constricted. He walked back and stood over Roy. Roy got up. He staggered a little.

"Coming, Gord. I was just resting." His speech was beginning to blur, his tongue hesitating over the words a little too long.

"You had to spoil it," said Gord. "I gave you this break and you had to spoil it. You can't stay off the bloody bottle for a minute, can you?"

"Nothing's spoiled, Gord. Just had a drink. Just had a *regmaaker*. That's all. Nothing wrong."

"How much have you had?"

"Just a sip, Gord. No need to get annoyed. Just a sip."
Gord took the bottle out of Roy's side pocket. It was
half empty.

"A sip," he said. "You booze artist. It's really got you,
hasn't it? It's really got you by the shorts."

He heard Elias come up and stand behind him. Roy held
out his hand.

"Give it to me, Gord. I won't touch it until we're finished.
Promise, I'll put it in my pocket and I won't touch it."

"You couldn't," said Gord. "It'll burn a hole in your
pocket. You couldn't leave it." He threw the bottle into the
long grass beside the path, heard it slither and slide
through the grass and clink on the earth.

"I'll pay you for that," he said. "Now come on. You're
drunk but perhaps the walk'll sober you up."

"You don't speak to me like that, Gord," said Roy. He
had all the pugnacity of the drunk now. He was ready
for a fight now. He stood in front of Gord and his mouth
was twitching.

"You don't call me a drunkard. You don't call me that in
front of a kaffir. You watch it, Gord. You don't call me anything at all anytime and you don't abuse me in front of a
kaffir."

"I'm an old man, Roy," said Gord. He was suddenly
very, very tired and sick of the whole business and anger
was searing right through him. "I'm an old man but I'll
break your bloody neck, if you give me any trouble. Now
get your bloody gun and come on."

He turned and walked down the path, quickly, feeling
his anger hard inside him, so hard that he wanted more

than anything just then to hit Roy, very hard. He picked
up his rifle and when he looked back Roy was on his
knees in the grass, feeling for the bottle.

He and Elias walked down the slope and after a while
Roy caught up with them. He walked behind them without speaking and now and again he would stumble and
Gord guessed he had finished the bottle. The sun was well
up and they could feel it through their shirts. They started
to sweat. It was going to be a hot day. They went down
into the dry riverbed at the bottom of the valley, trying
to keep to the shade of the overhanging bushes. The riverbed was flat stones and fine gray sand and smooth pebbles,
heavy to walk in, but at least it had shade. On one long
stretch the high thorn trees met over the riverbed and the
stones under the trees were white with guinea-fowl droppings. It would be a good place to come and shoot roosting
guinea fowl at night, thought Gord, with a .22 against the
moon.

Even though it was only donkey they were going after,
he felt the old excitement. He just wished he had somebody else, anybody else, except Roy. He had thought it
would be a mistake to bring Roy and he had been right.
He had no confidence in Roy at all. He looked back. The
heat was sweating the liquor out of Roy and his face was
blotchy and shining with sweat.

He was looking very bad. He was making very heavy
going of it. He held the shotgun as though it was a walking
stick.

He tried to stop thinking about Roy. He walked ahead
with the Swazi. It was really hot now, and windless down

[131]

in the river bed. The Christmas beetles had started their high electric buzzing. Through the branches the sky was very blue and cloudless. Right about them two black specks flew in wide circles: *lammervanger* eagles from the cliffs across the valley. Their high harsh cries drifted down from the sky.

Forty years ago he had walked along a riverbed like this with a good man beside him, forty years and three thousand miles ago. They had shot a hartebeest on a flat near the Tana River, he and his cousin Evelyn: it had fallen near a marula tree, and they decided to come back at sunset and wait for the lions they knew were in the area, getting up in the tree and shooting down on the lions from fifty yards. But they had one drink too many before leaving their camp that afternoon, and when they walked up to the tree it was already almost dark. They were thirty yards from the dead hartebeest when the six lions which had been lying in the grass around the carcass got up and walked growling towards them. It was almost too dark to see, but the lions were against the last light. Gord got one, and Evelyn shot another that came with a rush — at five yards, standing as straight and unworried as though he were on a range, the long Mannlicher spitting three rounds so quickly that the echoes rolled across the flats like one shot. The other lions turned away, running back into the bush along the river. By now it was fully dark and Gord and Evelyn lit the lantern they had brought and walked back to camp. The lions came out of the bush and followed them back to the camp, keeping just out of the lantern light, grunting and growling as they quested back and forth in the dark. They were young lions (Gord and Evelyn could see their spoors the next morning) and lacked the courage for a frontal charge into the light. So they contented themselves with harrying tactics, making short rushes, coughing and grunting and pulling up short, and when Gord and Evelyn were back at the camp the lions went down to the riverbed and roared all night. That was a good night, thought Gord. That was living then. Evelyn. There was a shot. There was a man who could shoot. He wished Evelyn was with him now. Well, there's no use wishing that. But I still wish it. He remembered Evelyn very well now. It was as though he had seen him yesterday. That dreadful hat he wore, floppy gray felt, greasy, not at all like the hats white hunters are supposed to wear, not one of those smart hats with a leopard-skin band. Just a dirty greasy floppy gray felt hat with a wide brim and the eyes under it the hardest blue you ever saw, eyes netted in fine sun-wrinkles, that never missed anything at all, so that the Masai called him "The Man Who Has the Eye of an Eagle." He stopped hunting finally, with his eyes still as good as ever, and bought a small tobacco farm in Rhodesia, and did quite well out of it: and then one day he was trolling for tigerfish from an overhanging rock on the Zambesi when a big crocodile came out of the muddy river and grabbed him by the foot and pulled him, bumping and scrabbling and scraping, into the river. Evelyn was a strong man and he got his fingers in the crocodile's eyes and it let him go and he struggled out onto the rock, and while he was lying there gasping the crocodile came back again, being by now probably very angry as well as hungry, and got

[133]

him by the same injured foot and pulled him under again. This time it was really determined and tried to push him into the mud overhang of the river bank, but Evelyn went for its eyes again (Gord often wondered how he had kept his presence of mind, down below the surface of the muddy river, down in the dark with his foot being chewed off) and came loose and crawled up the bank with his right foot a chewed stump. They got him to the hospital in Salisbury in time to stop him from bleeding to death, after the local doctor had done some rough surgery, and there they took off part of his leg. It never healed, though, and a year later he went down to Johannesburg, where they took off another slice, and a year after that he went down to Port Elizabeth, where he had heard there was a good surgeon, and had the third amputation. His heart just stopped beating one night. The surgeon said it was a great pity because the stump was healing nicely.

They came out of the riverbed where a stand of small Port Jackson willows sloped down to the dry bed. Through the trees they could see the donkeys grazing at the lower end of the valley, near the fence. The men walked up under the trees, their boots crunching on the fallen leaves and brittle seed pods, and the donkeys heard them even at that distance and stopped grazing, flickering their ears toward the sound. When the three men came out from the shadow of the trees the donkeys turned away, going down the valley.

"Let's go," said Gord. He put the butt of the Lee-Enfield against his hip and fired a round into the sky. The donkeys jumped at the gunshot and trotted down the valley, all bunched together, tails whisking. There were about thirty of them, led by the big black jack, the biggest donkey Gord had ever seen.

"Come on," he said. They began walking very fast across the flats. The donkeys were spread out along the fence now. They were nervous and all trying to get farthest away from the three men coming through the grass. One string of four donkeys broke away left and ran up the fence, away from the donga with the thorn wall. Gord lay down, resting on his elbows, and shot the leading donkey so that it fell in the game path along the fence. The others turned back, but one broke away again and tried to run back down the valley, sensing a trap, and the main pack, milling against the fence, turned and broke too, spreading out over the flat, in a real panic now. Gord stayed on his elbows and shot the leader at three hundred yards, the soft-nose bullet making a solid *thwack!* as the donkey came down on his chest and rolled over, kicking up the dust. Gord stood up and beat the dust from his clothes and thumbed two more cartridges into the magazine and they went on up the slope, cutting over the shoulder of the low hill.

They walked up three abreast through the grass. Roy was sweating and panting a little, holding the shotgun with both hands, out in front of him. The Swazi Elias was grinning now, sweat on his face, the shotgun held ready, another cartridge in his right hand, the hammer on the choke barrel back. I hope he's got the safety on, thought Gord. They went over the hill. The donkeys were huddled together just over the rise. They had stopped as soon as the men were out of sight. Now they panicked again, wheeling

and galloping down into the donga and up it, through the
sand and stones and small prickly pear, toward the thorn
wall. They turned the elbow of the donga, which was here
very narrow and steep-sided, and the donkeys were coming
back down towards them, really frightened now, heads
shaking and hooves clattering on the stones.

"Now," said Gord. "Now." He knelt and fired, taking the
front left donkey and moving across the pack, firing and
working the bolt as fast as he could, the full clip held ready
in his left hand against the stock, the Lee-Enfield thudding
back against his shoulder and the cordite smell strong on
the hot air and the spent brass cartridge cases clinking on
the stones and the high *tweeeennnnggg* of lead ricocheting
from the rock walls on the donga. And then the rifle was
empty and he was getting the new clip in and the Swazi
was firing his 16-bore — *bawhammm . . . bawhammm . . .
bawhammm* right beside him, so that his ears sang — and
over to the right he saw with one eye Roy fumbling with
the broken-open shotgun, trying to get a shell into the
chamber with the donkeys almost on him in their blind
panic. Gord got the new clip in and fired right over the
Swazi's head, dropping a donkey skidding in front of Roy,
who had left the shotgun now and was lying on his side in
the sand, his arms covering his head. Then the last of the
donkeys were through, jumping over Roy, and Gord's rifle
was empty and the Swazi had stopped firing because they
were too far for the shotgun. He broke the gun and un-
loaded it, dropping the thick green cartridges into his
pocket, and shaking his head. Gord walked across and
touched Roy with his foot. Roy uncurled and stood up.

There was dust on his face and clothes and sand dribbled from the muzzle of the bore when he picked it up. Gord took the gun from him without speaking and turned to look up the donga and although he was expecting it to be ugly he had never guessed how ugly it would be, twenty dead and dying donkeys and the smell of hot donkey blood and fresh manure making bright green steaming trails among the dead donkeys and the long glistening purple and red sausage of entrails looping across the back and flanks of a big jenny which had taken two charges from the Swazi's 16-bore at ten feet and then slipped and rolled with her legs entangled in her own viscera. He put a fresh clip in the Lee-Enfield and finished the wounded animals. Already the donga was droning with flies. Gord walked to the overhang and sat down. He felt sick to his stomach and his hands were trembling. He watched the Swazi sharpening his skinning knife on a flat stone and wanted to get out of the donga. Roy walked over to him. It was very quiet in the donga now, between the high walls, with only the droning of the flies and sometimes a far-off bird cry from the bush outside. Roy's feet sounded very loud in the gravel. Gord felt that his senses had suddenly become sharpened, painfully acute, so that he could hear each individual grain of sand crumble beneath Roy's boots, hear the clink of each hobnail against the gravel. Keeping his eyes down, he could see the grain on the cracked leather, the weave of the dirty trousers and behind this, like a monstrously enlarged photograph, the dead donkeys, gray-white tongues lolling from open mouths over yellow teeth, eyes glazing in the sun, stiff sparse bristle-like hair stirring in the hot dry eddies of wind, fat blue lice obscene globules on the distended bellies, shining flies like crawling scabs on the black wounds, the blood dark and thick as molasses, setting on the baking stones.

Roy stopped. Gord stood up. He still held the Lee-Enfield and even now he remembered he still had a cartridge in the chamber. He worked the bolt and caught the cartridge in his left hand, holding the next cartridge down against the spring of the magazine with his thumb so that breech closed empty.

"Gord," said Roy. Gord did not look at him.

"Gord. I'm sorry about that, Gord. Gun jammed, Gord." He had been badly frightened and all the liquor had gone out of him and left him shaking and washed-out in the heat. Gord took the shotgun from him and broke it and took the shells out. He smelled the chambers. There was no powder smell. He cocked the hammers and tried the action, easing the hammers down with his thumb. He looked at Roy.

"You bloody fool," he said, very softly. "You had the safety on."

He leaned the shotgun against the rock and pulled his hat lower over his eyes.

"If you want to make enough for a drink out of this you better give the boy a hand with the slaughtering," he said. He picked up the rifle and walked out into the sun. The Swazi was squatting beside a donkey. He had the skin half off and he was doing things inside the rib cage with his arms red to the elbows.

"I'm going after the animals that got through," said

Gord. "Then I'll go to Baas Hammersley's and tell them to send the truck for the meat. Baas Roy will help you until I come back. Have you got another knife?"

Elias nodded. There was a blood smear across his cheek. "*Ewe,* Baas Gord."

Gord turned and walked out of the donga and up the slope. He did not look back but went on walking very quickly through the long grass as though something was following him. But when he got out of the long grass and on the open flats the only thing left with him was his shadow. The sun was very high now and the shadow was a small twisted shape at his feet.

20

There was a quiet insidious rain coming down on the town. It was the rain which came from the sea with the regular southeast wind. It came softly over the hills and drifted over the roofs in swaying veils of damp and depression, gently eroding, laying the dust and muffling the echoes and hanging flaccid on the leaves. It was a mist and drip rain.

Gord came down in the evening. The rain was still coming in from the sea. The narrow main street was very quiet with the street lights reflected in the shining wet cars parked under the trees. He pulled the Ford in against the curb and walked quickly in the rain across the street and into the Royal Hotel. He passed the main lounge at the rear of the hotel. He did not feel like the bar tonight. The back room was very small with a bare floor and a few cheap cigarette-marked tables and uncomfortable chairs. There was a serving hatch through to the bar. When Gord came in the serving hatch was open and he could see into the bar. A waiter was standing at the window looking out at the rain. He came across and Gord ordered a

*Commando brandy and water. The waiter spoke through
the hatch and the barman put his head through and saw
Gord.*

"Hullo, Gord," he said. "Somebody was looking for you."

"Oh no," said Gord. "Not him. Not Roy."

*"I'll send him through," said the barman. He brought
Gord's drink and shut the hatch. The waiter carried the
drink across to Gord and went back to the window. He
seemed to find the rain quite absorbing.*

*Gord wished he had stayed at home. The lounge was
very depressing. There were four or five other people in the
lounge and they were all very depressing. In the far corner
a fat man was drinking with a fat young woman. She was
wearing one of those crimpy nylon dresses that are almost
transparent. The dress was pale green and her thick arms
were pouchy with fat and also greenish under the light.
She and the man were drinking very earnestly and they
were both almost drunk.*

*A policeman Gord knew was drinking a few tables away.
He was a big man with wavy ginger hair. He was drinking
double brandies. He was off duty and wearing a really
ugly blazer, blue with vertical yellow stripes. The policeman was a really hard drinker. Gord had been on a leopard
hunt with him a few years ago. A leopard had been killing
sheep around the district and after it had killed about three
hundred the farmers demanded some action; so this captain had taken twenty constables and two packs of jackal-
dogs up into the hills. They had driven up in two big
trucks, a pack of dogs in each truck. The dogs were from
different farms and as soon as the truck tailgates were*

lowered the dogs went for each other and it took ten
minutes of kicking and clubbing to separate them, by
which time the leopard must have got well away, and after
the dogs had been separated they had to give first aid to a
young constable who had been badly bitten in the fight,
and somebody had to drive him back to the hospital for an
anti-tetanus injection. By the time all this was over the
police captain had lost all interest in the hunt. He sent the
dogs and men off down the kloof, telling them to circle and
beat across it, posting men with .303 rifles on the high
places, and then he sat down on the tailgate of the truck
and got drunk in the sun. The men came back later in the
afternoon, without the leopard, but with a calf which had
been shot by mistake. This annoyed the captain very much
and he said some hard things to the constable responsible.
He and Gord had had a few drinks together since then but
Gord was a little afraid of any man who drank as heavily
as the policeman. He thought it might be catching. So this
evening he just smiled and said hello to the policeman, who
was drinking with two friends anyway, and hoped he
could let it go at that.

Then the door between the lounge and the bar opened
and Roy came in. He looked around for Gord and when he
saw him he walked across and sat down. He put his glass
on the table, slopping a little brandy. He was very drunk,
drunker than Gord had seen him for a long time. He had
been spending his share of the donkey money.

"Gord," he said. "I want to see you. I want to speak to
you, Gord."

"There's nothing to talk about, Roy," said Gord.

"You're still annoyed with me, Gord, aren't you?"

"Just let's forget about it. That's all over now. No good
raking it up again."

"But I didn't want you to get the wrong impression,
Gord. That's what I didn't want, the wrong impression.
We've been friends for a long time, Gord."

"Have we?" said Gord. He signaled to the waiter and
ordered another brandy. Roy's glass was empty and Gord
felt him watching.

"One, Baas?" asked the waiter, looking at Roy.

"Yes," said Gord. The waiter went away and brought
back one drink. Roy ordered himself a drink. He looked
hurt.

"I know you thought I let you down, up there in the
bush," said Roy. He was trying to be very noble and dignified.

"Didn't you?" asked Gord. He was beginning to feel
very annoyed.

"I'm sorry you think that of me, Gord," said Roy. He was
starting to become emotional. "I'm sorry you think that of
me. I really am. You know my condition."

"I know your condition all right," said Gord. "I know
your condition too bloody well."

"The sun brought it on. I thought I was going to have
an attack."

"Of what?" asked Gord. "The D.T.'s?"

"That's not very decent, Gord. You know that's not very
decent of you."

"Please go home, Roy," said Gord. "I really don't want
to speak to you or drink with you or anything with you."

"*I just want you to understand, Gord. I just don't want you to think I let you down up there.*"

"*All right,*" said Gord. "*I don't think you let me down up there. Does that make you happy?*"

"*I thought I was going to have an attack. I could have a hemorrhage at any time, you know. A fatal hemorrhage. What would you have done then?*"

"*Done the job a bloody sight quicker than we did, with you farting about all over the place,*" said Gord.

"*I hope you never have a tumor, Gord,*" said Roy. He was now being very forgiving and Christian. He finished his drink very quickly and ordered another.

"*Having one, Gord?*"

"*I'll get my own, thanks,*" said Gord.

"*You don't have to be like that, Gord,*" said Roy. "*You don't have to be like that. I thought you were different. Now you're being like all the others.*"

"*I'm sorry,*" said Gord.

"*There's not much left for me,*" said Roy. "*You know that? There's not much left for me.*"

"*There's not much left for most of us,*" said Gord. He was beginning to feel sorry for Roy again. He looked at him sitting there slumped in the chair with his twitching lips and shabby blazer and cracked shoes and trembling hands, and over Roy's shoulder, stretching down the long road behind him, he saw the bright new cars and the good jobs and the less than good jobs and the downright dirty jobs and the house in the suburbs and the children and the wife, and the lies and the tears and the brave resolu-

tions and the broken resolutions and hope and pride and belief all strung along the narrowing avenue of years leading to this dirty third-rate lounge in a third-rate hotel in a defeated town.

"There's only my mother," said Roy. He was very sentimental now. "There's only the old lady. She's all that keeps me going. Sometimes I feel like knocking myself off, ending it all."

"Who's stopping you?" asked Gord. *He had felt sorry for Roy until he brought his mother in. He should have left his mother out of this, thought Gord. He should have left her out of this and he would have had me feeling sorry for him again.*

"It would kill her," said Roy. "She's in Bloemfontein. It would kill her. I've often thought of it but it would kill her. I've got to stay on here for her." *His voice was husky with emotion.*

"Oh, shut up, Roy," said Gord. "Please shut up. I'm tired of you. I'm tired of everything about you."

"You don't believe I'll do it," said Roy. *He was very drunk and near to tears. This was his last chance to prove that he had anything left at all and Gord was not giving the right answers.*

"You'll see, the whole lot of you. You don't believe me, do you? You don't think I've got it in me, do you? I have. I have got it."

"All right," said Gord. "You have got it. Does that make you happy? You have got it and you're going to kill yourself and give us all a bit of peace."

"*Just do it when I'm off duty,*" *said the policeman, who had been leaning back in his chair to listen. His friends laughed.*

"*Just don't do it when I'm on duty,*" *said the policeman, and this time he laughed too.*

"*You shut up,*" *said Roy. He was quite brave when he was drunk. "You shut up."*

The policeman, who was really a very big man, with large square hands and very wide shoulders, looked surprised. He pushed his chair back and stood up.

"*Don't worry about him,*" *said Gord. "You don't have to take any notice of him."*

The policeman sat down again.

"*Tell him to keep quiet, then,*" *he said. "He's a nothing. Tell him not to look for trouble."*

"*I could handle him,*" *said Roy. "I could handle him." He turned in his chair and looked threateningly at the policeman.*

"*You couldn't handle anyone,*" *said Gord. "You'd better go home."*

"*In my time,*" *said Roy. "I'll go home in my time. I'll do anything I want in my time. I don't need him or you or anyone to tell me when to do anything. You think I won't do it, don't you?*"

"*I thought we were off that subject,*" *said Gord. He was feeling the two brandies now.*

"*I could do it tonight,*" *said Roy. There were tears in his eyes. "I could do it tonight."*

Gord stood up and walked out of the lounge and through the crowded front bar and out the front door of the hotel.

Outside the air was fresh and cool. The rain had stopped and there were high wispy clouds with the new moon behind them. A little wind had come up and was shaking the rain from the trees. Gord walked across the road and under the dripping trees and opened the driver's door of the Ford and slid in behind the wheel. He leaned across and unlocked the glove box and took out the big Colt. He ejected all the cartridges out into his hand and dropped them in his pocket and got out, shutting the door carefully behind him, and walked back across the street to the hotel. He held the Colt by the barrel, holding it up against his thigh so that they did not notice it when he walked through the bar. Roy looked up when he came back into the lounge.

"Gord —" he said, and then Gord put the big Colt on the table, sliding it across the scarred wood towards him so that the revolver swiveled on the cylinder and came to rest with the butt beside Roy's hand.

"Go on," said Gord. "Pick it up."

It was very quiet in the lounge. The waiter stopped looking out at the rain and the policeman sat back in his chair, watching Roy.

"No, Gord," said Roy. "Please." He sat staring at the big gun.

"You wanted it," said Gord. "You wanted to do it. You wanted to talk about it. So now I'm helping you."

It was very quiet in the small lounge. A moth was jerking around the ceiling light, clinking against the frosted glass shade. The waiter stood with his tray held before him, against his chest, like a shield. Somebody laughed very loudly in the front bar, the sound coming through the closed hatch, and then Roy began to cry, the tears running down his cheeks in two streams. He sat there crying silently and Gord picked up the Colt and walked out, all the anger gone out of him, all the irritation gone right away out of him, and only shame sitting like a hot pain in his stomach. The policeman followed him out. Gord waited for him on the stoep.

"You shouldn't have done that, Gord," he said.

"You didn't interfere," said Gord. "Why didn't you interfere? He just got on my nerves." He wanted someone to share the blame now.

"I saw the gun was empty," said the policeman. "I saw the chamber when you put it down."

"I knew he wouldn't do it," said Gord. "I knew he wouldn't do that." They walked across the road to the Ford. Gord got in and the policeman leaned through the window.

"If you knew he wouldn't, Gord, why'd you empty the gun first?" he asked.

"I don't know," said Gord. He pulled out from under the trees and drove up the street. In the rear-view mirror he could see the policeman standing in the street with the light from the hotel on him. Gord drove out of town and hit the dirt road and changed down to second for the pull up to the house. He was wondering why he had taken the cartridges out of the Colt. He thought about it all the way home and when he was in bed he lay awake thinking about it. He couldn't understand it very well but he felt that by doing that he had spoiled something in himself.

21

THE winter came cold and dry and went, and then the
spring rains came and on the hills around the town the red
earth grew a green stubble, new grass and spindly *maer-
man* plants, and the air had every day the feel of the sea
in it and the wind coming up the valley brought the sound
of the road gang right into the town. They were working
through hard red rock now and blasting every day. The
blasting made flat thuds which could be felt in the town,
the air going away and then coming back suddenly, slapping the windows.

There was a lot of rain that spring, and a lot of wind
with it. There were puddles in the streets most days and
the walls of the houses and the wheels and bodies of the
cars and trucks were always muddy. During the days,
between showers, the sun came out and it was warm out of
the wind, in the lee of the houses; but the wind coming
over the hills was sharp and wet and at night the streets
were wet-blown and cold.

In the house on the hill they lived mostly in the kitchen.
It was warmer there. They kept the fire going all the time,

building it up at night. They liked the kitchen because all they had left now was the kitchen: most of the lounge furniture had gone, except some hard chairs and the table; so had the display cabinet with the blue-and-white dinner set; so had the carved hat stand in the hall; the stinkwood chest. All they had left was the kitchen and the bedroom and Gord's guns and the picture of the young man beneath the elephant tusks. The other rooms of the house were silent and dusty and empty and the passage echoed when they walked down it. So now at the winter's end they had retreated to the kitchen, moving only between it and the bedroom, going out by the back door when they had to, avoiding the silent high empty hall and the young man under the tusks and the closed doors of the empty rooms, guiltily.

There was a small garden behind the kitchen, a plot of good black earth which Gord had spaded and fertilized and weeded, and Julia grew carrots and spinach and cabbage and long green runner beans and very hot white radishes. In the early morning there were always birds in the garden, drab mousebirds, rat-like with their spiky tails; bright spreeuws, wary doves, noisy weaver birds, the yellow vinks. Once a hare came through the fence and sat right outside the window, sitting up very straight with his ears erect while he ate cabbage, and one morning Gord found a duiker's prints in the garden. That pleased him more than anything he could remember for a long time. He came back into the kitchen and made some coffee and sat drinking it and looking out at the garden and thought of the duiker walking in his garden during the night.

"I'm very happy," he said to Julia. "I'm very happy now. I don't know why. I shouldn't be, but I am. I'm glad that duiker came in. I think I'll make a little place for him in the fence, a place for him to come through. He had to scrape through last night. I found a bit of his fur on the wire."

"We can't afford to keep a duiker," she said, watching him.

"We can afford it," he said. "We couldn't afford it before but now we can. It doesn't make any difference now."

"You could shoot it," Julia said. "I could do a lot with a duiker." She was still watching him.

"No," he said. "I don't want to do that. I don't think I'll shoot anything any more. I've done enough killing. I don't want to do any more killing. There's too much killing in this country now."

"There was more when you were a young man," she said.

"That was a different sort," he said, looking at the duiker prints in the garden.

"It was the donkeys, wasn't it?"

"Them and everything. Them and everything else. I don't think it was them alone."

He sat looking out of the window. He had lost weight during the winter and he no longer felt well at all, not early in the morning nor late at night nor anytime.

"It's not so bad when you're doing it," he said. "I mean the shooting and the hunting and the killing. You and people like you. You know what you are like and though you kill a lot of lion or buck or elephant or anything you don't think it's bad because you know that you're all right, you're

[151]

not going to spoil the country, because you know when to stop, and then one day you realize that there's no more people like you and all of a sudden everything has turned bad, so you hate to think about it, and you can't face the bush again. When it gets very bad you can't even face your own memories again, and you feel like you did when you were a child and had done something you were really ashamed of. Then it's terrible and you turn around and around like a bird in a cage but there's nowhere to go. It is worst in the very early morning and late at night and also at midday."

"It was the donkeys," she said. "I shouldn't have let you do it. It wasn't the sort of thing you should have done. It was kaffir's work."

He looked at her, surprised. He had never heard her say a thing like that before.

"It was. It was them," she said.

"Please let's stop talking about the donkeys," he said. He got up and walked to his room and put on his old jacket and his hat and went down the hall, past the gun rack, without looking at the guns. He had not cleaned them for months and the dust was thick on them.

He went out the back door and around the house and walked down the road, away from the town. The air was still cool and the dew was still sparkling on the fence beside the road. Over the rise he could see the road gang starting work and smell the hot tar. They were almost in the town now. Already, in anticipation of the new business which the good road would bring, one of the big oil companies had opened a six-pump service station on the edge

of the town. He stood on the rise a long while, watching
the road gang, looking at the far blue mountains with the
sea beyond them, at the end of the black road, puddled
with shining water mirages, arrowing through the gray-
green bush. He walked slowly down the road. The prickly
pears were blooming, bright orange flowers capping the
fleshy young fruits. They were immature prickly pears and
the leaves were still a bright fresh green. He walked very
slowly down the road, feeling the loved land all around
him, seeing every plant, every insect, every bird, feeling
the wind from the sea and watching the clouds building up
over the mountains. Mornings like this he and Stuart would
go down to the winding river below the old farmhouse to
catch eels, *palings* they called them, in the cool quiet
opaque green water under the willow trees. One morning
the dogs — they had a crossbred ridgeback and a boerbul —
had put up a rooikat. They often wondered what a rooikat
was doing down there, far from his usual run. The rooikat
climbed a boerboon tree and sat snarling and spitting, his
tasseled lynx ears flat on his beautiful head, his eyes yellow
and angry and frightened and hard as glass, and they had
an impasse. If even one of them ran back to the house for
the shotgun (and it was a mile uphill) the rooikat would
jump for it. They could see that by the way he crouched,
his back arched, like strung bow. He would probably jump
on the boy who stayed, ignoring the dogs. He kept his eyes
on the boys all the time, hardly noticing the dogs, which
were howling and running halfway up the tall boerboon
tree before falling back. And if both boys went, he would
take the dogs. They were very young and inexperienced

dogs and a grown rooikat would give them a very bad time.

"We'll have to get him down," said Stuart.

"Yes," said Gord. His stomach was fluttering with excitement and some fear. Stuart cut two thick milkwood sticks and gave Gord one.

"You watch out," he said, "and don't *donner* the dogs by mistake."

He went around the tree, the rooikat following him with its angry eyes, and then he swung himself up, very quickly, and rammed the sharp end of the stick hard under the rooikat's bobtail. The cat came out of the tree with a wild scream and landed skidding on the dry leaves, back arched, ears down and lips back wide: and then the dogs were rolling with it, and Gord was trying to hit the rooikat without braining the dogs, which was not easy, and it was all dust and leaves and fur flying spittle. In the melee Gord took a wild swipe and broke his stick over the boerbul's head by mistake, and the dog let the rooikat go and walked off, weaving, into the bush. The ridgeback broke off the engagement then and the rooikat bounded off into the trees along the river.

They found the groggy boerbul and washed his bloodied head and gave him some water at the river and after a little while he was able to walk home with them. Stuart tried hard to be angry but he kept smiling to himself and finally he laughed out loud. The boerbul, walking ahead with dried blood on his fur and probably a bad headache, looked back reproachfully at them.

Gord, walking down the new-graded dirt road in the

early morning, remembered all this very clearly now, more clearly than he had for years. I am getting old, he thought. That was fifty years ago and I remember it better than I remember things that happened last week. But then nothing that happened last week was as interesting or even as real as that rooikat in the tree fifty years ago. He looked down the road, with the air just beginning to quiver with heat over the red dust, and he saw the boerbul look back at him with reproach, and he laughed, throwing his head back and closing his eyes, he laughed and laughed. The boerbul had lived for many years after that, getting old and irritable, and one afternoon it had died in its sleep under his father's cane chair on the front stoep. The ridgeback, which was a much more impetuous dog, had been killed shortly after the rooikat affair, when it unwisely cornered a big yellow Cape cobra in the feed store behind the house. The ridgeback was very excitable and not afraid of anything, not even a seven-foot angry cobra, and he had gone in barking and broken the snake's back, but not before it had bitten him several times.

He had known a good many dogs. Dogs varied as much as people. He had known some good dogs and some very bad dogs indeed. In the bush a good dog was worth a lot and a bad or a cowardly dog was quite useless and sometimes very dangerous.

He went on down the road. The roar and clatter of the gang was very near now and he could see the dust over the tops of the bushes. He came around the bend and the noise broke over him like a breaker. He stopped and watched the bulldozers and the big mechanical shovel taking mouthfuls of earth and then he went up off the road, walking around the gang through the bush. He was a little afraid of the big machines. He was afraid of being tainted. Even here in the bush he could smell the hot tar and the thick exhaust fumes and the peculiar stink of splintered rock, something you couldn't quite describe, but which got you right at the back of the nose so you wanted to sneeze.

When he was past the road gang he came back onto the new road and walked along it. The tar was still unmarked and shining and the loose chips along the shoulder were hard and sharp beneath his shoes. The road went straight away from him like a corridor through the thick thorn, with the new-cut earth and rock still looking raw, not yet softened with new growth. He walked along it for a mile and wished he could appreciate it but he knew he never would. When he was tired he turned off the road and cut back across the hill to his house.

He stopped on a low koppie a hundred yards from the road, a small island of stones among the thorn, and looked back at the glistening road. Far away a small shape was moving, coming up the tar ribbon, and then he could hear the rattling roar of a big motorcycle with an open exhaust. He watched them pass, the goggled rider and his big noisy machine, and heard the engine cut at the road gang, swallowed up by the bigger noises. He thought of the miles he had bounced and jolted on his little Francis-Barnett over the unpaved roads, the potholed bush tracks which were national roads then. You rode a machine then. You really rode in those days. You didn't just sit in the saddle. You had to fight to stay on.

22

*O*n *his seventieth birthday Julia bought him a new shirt
and a half-jack of brandy and they sat and drank it with ice
and ginger ale in the kitchen, Julia in a fresh-washed dress
and he in his new shirt and with his old khaki trousers new-
laundered and knife-edge creased.*

*"I feel so good today," she said, "and you look like a
young man again. I feel as though something wonderful is
going to happen."*

"It would be about time," he said.

*"Remember when we were children how we believed
that the way you were on your birthday, that was the way
you would be for the rest of the year?" she said.*

"Then I'll be good today," he said.

*"Don't be good," she said. "Just be happy. That's all. Just
you be happy."*

She held up her glass. "To your birthday."

He bowed politely and lifted his glass. "To my birthday."

"I do feel wonderful," she said. "I've been remembering."

"*I thought I was the only one who did that.*"

"*As a rule. Because I don't worry about the past. I am happy today and I remember the happy times but I don't worry about them. You always wanted the happy times to stay and you made yourself unhappy when they didn't stay.*"

"*All right,*" he said. "*Let's change the subject.*"

"*I'm sorry,*" Julia said.

He poured himself another drink and added ginger ale. He was taking the brandy very slowly.

"*I found some old photos the other day,*" she said. "*I was going to show them to you but I thought it would make you discontented.*"

"*They probably would have.*"

"*There was one of you on that old motorbike of yours, that big one, with one of those leather caps they wore then, with a peak and earflaps, you know.*"

"*The old Ariel.*"

"*Yes. Remember how we were coming back to Port Elizabeth one day and at Addo there was a Chinaman at the filling station and he said that he'd start ten minutes behind us so we wouldn't have to drive in his dust? I always remembered him. A fat Chinaman with a car full of children and such a nice face.*"

"*Yes,*" he said. *He remembered. And on the Francis-Barnett, years before that, calling on a girl and doing a fancy turn on the gravel in front of the Hotel Elizabeth, with her mother and father and forty other guests watching, and the Francis-Barnett just slipping out from underneath him and sliding across the gravel, engine screaming, into the canna*

[159]

bed, and everyone, including the girl, laughing when they saw he wasn't hurt. Now he could not even remember her name. He was never any good with motorbikes or mechanical things, except guns, and somehow he never thought of them as mechanical things.

"We had a lot of fun on that old motorbike," she said. She looked almost girlish in the evening light. "I liked those picnics we had at Van Stadens Pass. That's such a pretty place. I hope it hasn't been spoiled."

"Yes," he said, thinking of the pass, the narrow twisting gravel road up through the deep kloofs with the tall trees all creeper-hung and wispy with Spanish moss. One night he had come through on a push-bike. It had rained earlier but when he got to the pass the rain had stopped and the stars were out. The road was muddy but because of the slope all the water had run off. He could hear it dripping and trickling into the kloof below. The road had no safety barrier, just a row of small white-painted stones. In the daytime when you drove through the pass you could see two or three twisted rusty wrecks lying among the high trees. This night he was pushing his bicycle up the road white in the starlight, when he heard a leopard cough in the bush below him. He felt his skin contract with fear and his stomach tighten and he could feel the sweat cold on his chest and back; but he had no gun, not even a revolver, and all he could do was keep pushing, slipping on the muddy road, trying not to run, while the leopard followed him right up to the top of the pass, so near to the road sometimes that he could hear it moving in the bush thirty feet away. On the top of the pass he jumped into the saddle

*and got off down the gently sloping dirt road at a speed
which he was privately convinced was a world record. He
had been through the pass once since then: the high trees
were mostly gone, the deep kloofs cleared to make way
for the huge pipes carrying water from the Churchill Dam
to Port Elizabeth, thirty miles away, and silver-gray pylons
strung the high-tension lines from hill to hill; and down at
the bottom of the pass, along the quiet brandy-colored
stream, there were public lavatories and concrete barbecue
pits and shower stalls and carefully grassed campsites and
in the middle, deep among the big trees, was a concrete
dance floor, strung with colored lights. "I don't think you'd
like it anymore," he said, thinking of the wire garbage
baskets on tall stakes, the litter of newspapers and cans and
bottles and in the summer the river dammed with water-
melon rinds, that almost mandatory debris of a South
African picnic.*

*"I suppose they want it that way," he said, and Julia
looked at him. "The picnickers. I was thinking of the picnickers," he said. "At Van Stadens."*

23

He had fished at the mouth with Stuart. The river was
a small one, and shallow, and the mouth was only fifty
yards wide and a few feet deep, but it came out into good
mussel grounds, and the grunter (although they called
them tiger on that part of the coast) and the steenbras
came in to feed pretty well during the winter; there were
a great many mussels there in those days. You stood in
the surf and as the waves scoured out the sand around your
feet you could feel the mussels thick as pebbles under you.
Standing waist-deep in the surf you could get a good cast
into the breakers. He smiled as he remembered how Stuart
had waded out neck-high one day with the surf dirty from
the river coming down, got in a good cast, and turned
shorewards to see two big yellow-belly sharks, seven-foot-
ers, swimming slowly between him and the shore, just their
small dorsal fins and the upper lobes of their tails showing. The surf was running big that day and every few
seconds a big swell would come right over Stuart and when
he saw the sharks he thought he was finished; but some-

*how they never smelled or sensed him, and in that dirty
surf there was no visibility at all, and they had swum on
up the beach.*

*The beach here was very wide and smooth, with high
white sand dunes inland. The road down to the beach
was very bad in those days and it was unusual to see any
other people on the whole sweeping stretch of sand, from
the rocks in the west to the headland hung with sea mist
in the east. It was a fine beach, with good surfing waves.*

"It's no good resenting it," said Julia.

"If they appreciated it," he said. "That's all. If people
just appreciated it."

"You want to keep things just as you like them," she said.
"Perhaps you are right. But perhaps you are not. We don't
know. How do you know they don't appreciate it?"

"I know," he said. "Believe me, I know."

"It is all for the best," she said.

"Are we back to that?" he said. "Are we back to that
again?"

"You have no faith," she said. "None at all. That's why
you are like this."

"Like what?"

"Unhappy. Unsettled. Bitter. You are an old man. You
should not be bitter."

"I haven't the strength to do anything about it," he said.
"I haven't the strength to change it and I haven't the
strength to accept it."

"We can be given strength. Our Lord gives us strength,

if we come to Him humbly and ask Him. I wish you would talk to Reverend Carey."

"I don't want to talk to Reverend Carey. I don't want to talk to anyone. You talk to Reverend Carey. You talk to him enough for both of us, in any case."

"I try to," she said. "I try to. I do pray for you, Gord."

"I don't want you to," he said. "It's insulting to be prayed for like that, in that way."

Julia got up and rinsed the glasses and then put them away. Outside the sun had gone and it was quite dark.

"Would you like supper now?" she said. Her face was quite peaceful and composed and suddenly so irritating that Gord felt a small pulse throbbing in his jaw. The feeling went as quickly as it had come and he felt so guilty that he touched her on the arm as she busied herself at the stove and when she turned he said, "I'm sorry, Julia," and she turned away and said, not looking at him, "I'm sorry too," and after that there was nothing else to say.

24

*I*T was eleven in the morning at the Royal Hotel. It was
the beginning of summer and the southeast wind was blowing hard and dry. The sky was a dirty gray, thin fast-mov-
ing clouds coming from the sea. Gord came in through
the side door, closing it quickly against the wind. He
walked up to the bar, putting his hat down carefully on
the glass-marked wood. He had come in to sell the Ford
and he wanted a drink first. He really resented wanting a
drink but there it was. He wanted one before he took the
car around. The knock in the engine was a loud clatter now
and he knew he was going to have a bad time. He put his
hand in his pocket and felt the few coins there, carefully.

"I'll have a Commando-and-water," he said. The barman poured him one, smiling. He thought it was very
amusing to see this old man drinking by himself. He was a
new barman Gord had not seen before. Gord had not been
to the Royal since the evening with Roy. He didn't want to
see Roy again. He had begun buying bottles of Commando
and taking them back to the house, drinking them in the

kitchen. Julia never said anything. He knew he was showing a weakness in his character but there was nothing he
could do about it. Julia had started going to church several
times a week now and her features had settled into a mask
of placidity and resignation which was beginning to worry
him. He found he was remembering Edith again, and wondering what it would have been like with her now. After
this time, he thought, watching the barman slice lemons
for the midday gins, after this time.

"Same?" asked the barman.

"What?" said Gord, and in the mirror behind the barman
he saw that he was leaning forward, his head on one side,
like an old man.

"Yes," he said, quickly, looking away. "Yes. Same again."

All of a sudden I'm old, he thought. On a December day
I'm old because I see it in a bar mirror. Some people grow
old gracefully. Others, like me, get it all in one go.

Now he just wanted to get out of the bar and sell the car
and get home, quickly, seeing as few people as possible.

25

The morning after Spion Kop it was raining. The trans-port wagons were back down the line. They had heard the firing all night, and in the morning they heard that Spion Kop had fallen. When it was light the first soldiers had come back, walking slowly through the rain, wet and splashed with mud by the cavalry which kept galloping past the rear, sodden pennants clinging to their lances, horses tired and breathing hard. They sat on the wagons and watched that parade of tired and dirty soldiers come back from the hills, many of them wounded and bandaged, and realized how it must have been up there on Spion Kop under the Mausers and the pom-poms. Then he saw a man he knew, a sergeant-major of the Fusiliers. He was a big man with a wide chest and buffalo mustaches and a voice like a lion's roar. He was fifty and had been in the army all his life and when he went up to Spion Kop he was as smart as if he were going on parade, swagger stick and all, and now he was coming back down the puddled road with his swagger stick gone and blood on his face, his spiked hel-

*met missing and his uniform torn at the knees and one put-
tee lose and trailing in the mud so that he kept giving a
funny little kick to untangle it from his other foot.*

*He walked past the wagon without seeing Gord and as
he walked he spoke quietly and reasonably to himself as
though he was explaining something. His mustaches had
lost their stiffness in the rain, and the ends were drooping
around the gently moving lips, giving a look of great and
ineffable sadness and bewilderment to the old man's face
under the muddled gray hair. He went on down the line,
an old man among the young soldiers. Gord looked after
him and shook his head, saying, "You poor old bastard, all
piss and wind last night, like a barber's cat, and now look
at you," and whipping up his team and taking the wagon
slowly through the retreating soldiers, who looked up re-
sentfully, but without the strength or the spirit, after Spion
Kop, to complain. Gord, in his twenties and untouched yet
by war or years or sadness, was sitting very tall on the
wagon box and no longer thinking about the old man but
only about getting the wagon loaded and back down the
lines befores the Boers started pushing.*

26

$\mathcal{N}$ ow in the Royal Hotel he saw himself in the mirror and thought of the sergeant-major and wondered whether he had ever got back to Wales and if he had, whether Wales was ever the same to him after Spion Kop — would any place ever be the same?

He finished his drink and went out into the wind and got into the Ford, sitting there for a while in the sun, wondering which of the town's two garages he should try first. He drove down the street and pulled in at the Star Garage. The Star was a small garage with three old fashioned hand pumps. The office was a red corrugated-iron building with new and recapped tires hanging on long pegs outside. He pulled the Ford in alongside the office and tapped the horn. The African attendant came out, wiping his hands on his greasy dark blue overalls.

"Is the manager in?" said Gord. "Is Mr. Engelbrecht in?"

"He's by the hotel now, Bass," said the attendant. "He's on lunch now, Baas."

Damn, Gord thought. He sat there, staring out through

the yellowing windshield and wondering what to do. I can go on to the new garage, he thought, but I know those big-town people will do me down. He listened to the klok-klok-klok in the idling engine and tried to make up his mind. The attendant stood respectfully beside the car.

Next to the Star Garage was the Ritz Café & Eating House. Two boys came out and stood on the pavement, looking up and down the street. They were about nineteen, dressed in blazers and flannels and carrying suitcases. They saw the Ford parked at the pumps and picked up their cheap suitcases and came over. They walked around the Ford and put the cases on the ground near the pumps. The attendant went back into the office.

"Good morning, sir," said the boy with fair hair. "You driving through?"

"No," said Gord. He did not like hitchhikers and even if he had any sympathy for hitchhikers he would not have liked them this morning.

"My friend and I are trying to get through to Fort Beaufort," said the boy. His friend nodded. They were both very fit-looking boys. The other one had mouse-colored hair and a bad skin around his mouth but otherwise he looked fit.

"Sorry," said Gord, "but I live here. I'm not going anywhere."

"We've got to get through this afternoon," said the boy. "We're catching the train to Bloemfontein from there. Tonight's train."

"Perhaps you'll get a lift," said Gord. He put the Ford into gear. "Best place is the bridge just outside of town."

"You run us through, we'll pay your petrol," said the second boy. He had an aggressive voice.

"No, thanks," said Gord. "Can't you hear this engine? It's just about gone. Sixty miles to Fort Beaufort would kill it."

The boys looked at each other.

"We'd be glad to pay you, sir," said the blond boy. He was smiling now and looking very boyish.

"No, thanks," said Gord. He took off the handbrake and the Ford rolled a little on the uneven concrete.

"We'll pay you your petrol and five pounds," said the mouse-haired boy. "We really must catch that train. Sir." He added the sir well afterwards. They smiled at each other and at Gord. Well, thought Gord, if she lasts, if she makes Fort Beaufort and back, I can still sell her, and be a fiver up. He switched off the engine and tapped the horn again. The attendant came out.

"Fill her up," said Gord. The boys watched without speaking while the attendant worked the hand pump, the yellow-brown gasoline filling the sight glass and then bubbling out again. The Ford took five gallons before she was full. The boys stood without speaking, smiling at each other, and when the tank was full and the attendant had replaced the screw cap on the petrol tank and wiped off the overflow, the blond boy paid him and they put their suitcases in the back and got in, the blonde boy in front with Gord and the mouse-haired boy in the back.

They drove out of town and up the dirt road, winding over the hill, and the Ford pulled quite well, and soon they were on the high flats, with the wind shaking the car and whipping dust from the road. When they were out of the hills Gord switched on the old Zenith radio and picked up a dance program from Grahamstown. He did not like carrying hitchhikers but otherwise he felt quite happy. If only she lasts until I get back, he thought. He wished he had had the oil checked. They were driving through open country now, thin grass and low thorn with few trees, and a long way between farms. The road had not been graded for a long time and the Ford with its bad shock absorbers was bouncing and crabbing on the loose corrugated surface. Gord used second a lot to get her up the long slopes and to hold her on the curves and after twenty miles she began boiling, rusty water squirting out from under the loose hood and blowing back over the windshield. When the temperature guage was in the red Gord switched off the engine and pulled the Ford off the road. In silence they could hear the radiator bubbling and the engine creaking and smell hot oil and steam. Over the tops of the scraggy bush they could see a new windmill, the blades still silver, facing into the wind.

"There's a pump over there," said Gord.

"Yes," said the blond boy. "You see that?" he said to the mouse-haired boy. "You see there's a windmill over there?"

"Well, that's interesting," said the mouse-haired boy. "Isn't that interesting?"

"We should come into the country more often," said the blond boy.

"We should," said the mouse-haired boy.

"All right," said Gord. "All right." He got out and got an

empty oil can from the boot and climbed over the fence and walked through the bush to the windmill. It was very hot and the wind was making a lot of noise in the thorn. He filled the can and came back through the bush, trying not to think about the boys. When he came back they were both sitting on the running board and the blond boy had got the Colt out of the glove box and was holding it between his knees. Gord put the can down, slopping water in the dust.

"What're you doing with that?" he said. "That's not yours."

"You're a bad old man," said the blond boy. "Isn't he?" to his friend.

"I'll say he is. A real bad old guy. Carrying guns and all."

"Now fill her up, Dad, because we're in a hurry."

"We're in a hurry," said the mouse-haired boy.

"You little bastards," said Gord. "You little bastards." He kicked the can over and water gurgled *gloop-gloop* into the hot sand. The mouse-haired boy jumped up and grabbed the can before all the water had gone and stood it up again.

He stood up holding the can and bumped Gord with his shoulder, crowding him. Gord stepped back to get his balance and swung at the boy but he was slow and the boy ducked, laughing, and the blond boy stood up, holding the gun, and said, "Watch it, Dad, you just watch it."

Gord went for the blond boy then, not worrying about the gun, and the mouse-haired boy grabbed him from behind, getting his arms through Gord's elbows and up behind his neck.

"Now then, Dad," he said, "now then." Gord stopped

straining and stood there, taking it. The boy let him go and stepped back, quickly.

"Now you be good, Dad," said the blond boy. "You put that water in the radiator."

"That will be the day," said Gord. "That will be the day."

He was sweating and shaking a little and ashamed of his weakness and he kept telling himself, "You're an old man, Gord, and these are fit youngsters." The words went around and around inside his head so he hardly saw the boys any more, just the long road with the sun and the wind on it and the windmill glinting about the gray bush and across the bush the blue mountains with the clouds coming over them from the sea.

"Well," said the blond boy, "so you're a tough old bastard, are you, Dad?" He picked up the can and lifted the hood and unscrewed the radiator cap. The rusty water had blown back over the engine when the radiator had boiled and the block was streaked brown. Gord saw it and thought, I'm lucky the block didn't crack, getting that water on it. But it was boiling water. Would it crack with boiling water? He couldn't think. He sat down suddenly on the bank and watched the boys fill the radiator. The mouse-haired boy went back over the fence and got another can of water. The second can filled the radiator and they got in the Ford, slamming the door hard. The engine took a long time to start and when the V–8 finally fired it ran rough, shorting out through the damp power leads and plugs. The blond boy pulled away noisily in first, the wheels spinning on the gravel, and the mouse-haired boy looked out of the window and waved. The Ford rolled on down the road and the dust

came up behind it and when it blew away the Ford had
gone and the sound of it was lost in the bush. The red-and-
yellow Shell oil can lay in the still grass beside the road
where the blond boy had thrown it.

27

At midday on Saturday the bar of the Royal Hotel was always crowded and too noisy to be pleasant. Gord stood on the corner, up against the wall, and wished he had not come down. He felt that way every time he came now but he couldn't stay in the house any more. The bar was long and narrow with swing doors at either end. One pair led to the urinals. The urinals had been cleaned that morning but the boy had used too much Jeyes Fluid so the whole bar stank of it. It was, at that, better than the usual smells which came through the swing doors.

"They find your car yet, Gord?" asked the barman. He was getting really friendly these days. He still thought it amusing to see an old man drinking in a public bar, but he was friendly.

"No," said Gord.

"These police," said the barman.

"Yes," said Gord. He did not want to talk about the car or anything else.

"Little bastards," said the barman. He went down the

counter and made two gin-and-tonics and came back to Gord.

"They'll get cuts for this," he said. He spoke as an authority. "They'll get four each. Car stealing's a very serious offense."

"If they catch them," said Gord. He no longer cared whether they caught them or not.

"If they catch them," said the barman. "Yes, if they catch them. That's the thing. They'll get cuts if they catch them. You know how they give it to them?"

"No," said Gord. "Can I have another brandy?" He wished the barman would shut up.

The barman poured him another brandy and pushed the water bottle across to him.

"They lay you across a bench," he said. "That's how they do it. They take your pants down and lay you across a bench and cover your backside with a cloth. That's so they don't break the skin. Couple of policemen hold you and a sergeant gives it to you with a riet. They call it a light cane but it's heavy enough, boy, it's heavy enough." He smiled inwardly at some remembered pleasure. "Man, you should hear them shout. You should just hear them."

The swing doors opened and the policeman came in. He was wearing his Saturday blazer. He came over to Gord and the barman poured him a brandy without waiting to be asked.

"We've found your car, Gord," he said. "They dropped it just outside Sandflats."

"I didn't think it would get that far," said Gord. "That's eighty miles. I never thought it would get that far."

"Perhaps you can get a lift over there," said the barman. He was very interested in Gord's car and the apprehension of the thieves. "And those ducktails, those *eendsterte,* did you catch them?"

"No," said the policeman, shortly.

"They'll get them," said the barman.

"Why did they ditch her?" asked Gord. He knew why but he wanted to hear it from someone else.

"They rode her rough, Gord," said the policeman. "They must have run her without any oil. The sergeant there by Sandflats says he started her up to bring her in and she's run a bearing so bad it sounds like it's coming through the block."

"That's fifty quid worth," said the barman. He shook his head. "That's at least fifty quid worth."

"Where's she now?" asked Gord.

"They left her about five miles outside Sandflats, on the Johannesburg road. They didn't want to drive her in and do more damage."

"That's true," said the barman.

"Well, thank you," said Gord. He was wondering how much it would cost to tow the Ford back.

"You going to leave her?" asked the policeman.

"I'll think about it," said Gord.

"You'll have to tell me," said the policeman. "You leave it there tonight, it'll be stripped to the chassis tomorrow unless I ask Sandflats to put a constable on it for the night."

"Give me a minute," said Gord. He went through to the telephone booth in the foyer. He got some small change from the hall porter and telephoned the Western Garage in Sandflats. He stood in the small booth and watched the street through the open doors of the hotel. When he got through to Sandflats he had to wait while they put him through to the garage and then wait again while they found the proprietor.

"Man, I've seen the car," said the proprietor. "The police asked me to have a look at it this morning, just in case I knew it, you know."

"Is it bad?" asked Gord. The telephone wires buzzed and hummed and there was the far-off sound of women talking.

"Man, yes." The proprietor's voice was very guttural. Western Province Afrikaans. He sounded like a stage Afrikaner.

"Man, yes. There's a very bad knock and she was run without water too, so the block's cracked as well."

"How much would you charge to tow her over here?" asked Gord.

"Over there? Man, you must be joking. The car isn't worth that much. I don't want to be rude, but the car isn't worth that much."

"Would you take her over?" asked Gord.

"Ag, man, I've got more old cars than I can handle now," said the proprietor. "I tell you, that one's not worth repairing. Cost you a hundred quid now, by the time you've finished."

"All right," said Gord. "Thank you."

He went back to the bar.

"Yes?" said the policeman.

"Nothing. She can stay there."

"Man, that's bad," said the policeman. "Perhaps somebody from this place will tow her home for you."

"No," said Gord. "Not anybody from here."

"I can't take the van," said the policeman. "You understand, I'd take the van across at night, but if it ever got out, well, I'd be really in the cart. It's government property."

"That's all right," said Gord. "Don't you worry about it."

"But I would, Gord," said the policeman. "You know I would."

"Forget it," said Gord. "I'm forgetting I had a car."

"Have another drink," said the policeman.

"It's a disgrace," said the barman.

"They'll get those little swine," said the policeman. "They've been doing this all the way down from Johannesburg."

"It'll be cuts for sure," said the barman, enjoying the thought. He flicked his towel.

"Like that. They'll sing another tune then."

"Please let's forget about my car," said Gord. "I'm tired of it."

"All right," said the barman. "All right."

"You talk too much," said the policeman. "Go'n bother someone else."

They had another drink. Gord felt the single note in his pocket and thought of Julia. She was at a church bazaar this morning. What the hell. He took out the pound and flattened it on the counter. The brandy was taking effect and he felt a little better now.

"Seen Roy lately?" asked the policeman. "Since that night?"

"No," said Gord. "Not since then. Is he still around?"

"He's still around, all right," said the policeman. He asked the barman: "Roy's still around, eh?"

"I'll say," said the barman. "He's around all right. Doesn't drink in here much any more, though."

"Is he working again?" asked Gord.

"In a way," said the policeman. He laughed. "In a way he's working very hard."

"Harder than he'd ever worked before," said the barman.

"He's working and drinking hard," said the policeman.

"He's got to work for his drink," said the barman, "and the harder he works the more he drinks."

"But he's got to work before he drinks," said the policeman.

"I'm not following," said Gord.

"He was on the bones," said the policeman. "You know that?"

"Yes?"

"He was on the bones of his backside and he took a room at Meyer's place, you know Koos Meyer's widow's place, down near the school."

"The boardinghouse."

"She calls it that," said the policeman. "Well, she took a fancy to him."

"He's not so bad, when he's cleaned up," said the barman.

"She took a fancy to him," said the policeman, "and she's putting him up for nothing. He helps her clean the place up, or something. Does her shopping and things."

"But what's he use for money?" asked Gord.

"He doesn't," said the policeman. "He does all his drinking at home. Bottle a day."

"She buys it here," said the barman. He didn't want to be left out. "She buys a dozen bottles every couple of weeks."

"That's Roy's price," said the policeman. "Bottle a time." He laughed.

"No," said Gord. "No."

"It is," said the policeman. "I promise you. That old woman was always *verskriklik jags,* man. She put old Koos in his grave. He just couldn't keep up."

"He won't look at her when he's sober," said the barman.

"That's not very often now," said the policeman. "She makes sure of that."

"I didn't think Roy had it in him," said Gord. He was feeling a little sick.

"He hasn't, hardly," said the policeman. "It's a delicate operation, man. She's got to give him just enough. Not too little, not too much." He laughed. He thought that was really funny.

"Like that advert, you've seen it. Not too little, not too much."

"It's a careful calculation," said the barman. "She keeps a tot measure beside the bed."

28

Roy Culworth lay on his bed in the big front double
room of Mrs. Meyer's boardinghouse. His tan topcoat was
hanging on a cup hook behind the door. The room was big
and high-ceilinged. The walls were cream oil paint and the
linoleum on the floor was green, with pink flowers. Around
the door it had been scuffed through and the backing
showed. Roy lay on the bed in his clothes but without his
shoes. It was very hot in the room at this time in the afternoon and the sour smell which soaked the whole house was
worse than ever. The curling strip of flypaper dangling
from the ceiling stirred slowly in some random breath, the
trapped flies buzzing erratically. Roy lay very still, listening
to the street outside. The breeze stirred the sashcord to
tap against the window frame and in the bright blue beyond he saw a streamer of cloud and the tops of some
far-off trees.

*At home they used to lie flat on their backs in the long
grass behind the house, staring up into the sky so long that*

in the end it seemed that they were looking down some infinite blue abyss. And on the swing you went right up towards the blue infinity so that it seemed that one day, with enough effort and heart and belief, you would go right up in a continuing arc, right into space and time and immensity and something inexpressible but so desirable that your heart squeezed within you. But the swing always came down again, as you knew it would, and you were in the sun-baked back yard again, with the rust-patched corrugated iron fence, the washing snapping in the wind like sails, the thin pale pepper tree, the water tank with a moss-edged puddle below the brass tap. On summer nights the bats came up from the dark valley behind the house and the little brown beetles flew in the grass and there was the scent of night-blowing flowers and the moon above the housetops was exciting and somehow a promise. Standing down in the dark garden you could look into the bright kitchen and it was like looking at a stage, his mother and the fat white-aproned cook girl silent-mouthing actors through the glass. And then childhood was something to hold on to for ever, there in the dark warm summer windblown garden with the moon over the houses and the world stopped at the high iron fence.

He lay on the bed and listened to the early afternoon sounds come up from the diningroom beneath, the clink of cutlery, the soft clash of plates, the high chatter of the servants, silly loud Xhosa girls from the location.

Footsteps on the stairs and doors opening and closing

[184]

and the boardinghouse settling down to its Saturday afternoon siesta. Somewhere down the passage a badly tuned radio was playing loudly. The wind came up in the hot afternoon and rattled the windows imperatively.

When this wind blew across the bay it brought in the stinging bluebottles with their long spiteful streamers and the lavender jellyfish and the conical sand snails came out in thousands to eat them stranded on the sands. The seagulls stood facing into the wind on the dirty sand flats near the oil installation and the wind piped in high wires and under the old wooden fishing jetty named after some long-forgotten Portuguese navigator. The coal dust from the bunker trucks blew down between the planks in a fine dark rain, threading patterns on the still green water going out through a forest of red-rusted girders to the wide and shining harbor.

Lying now on his unmade bed in this final room he could still remember well the walks along the beach with the blown sand whipping against bare feet, past the clustered sitting gulls, up over the high white dunes with the fine sand pluming from their crests, and through a gap in the customs fence to the jetty, dodging down through the old timbers under the eye of the railway policeman, then sitting, legs hooked over the rough girders, watching for the bull-headed gray mullet questing nervously through the shadowed, garbaged, limited sea. Overhead the ice trucks rumbled, and through the girders you could see the hull of a trawler, and beyond it, across the harbor, the big ships lay; but this place was yours, the mullet and the blacktail and the swarming yellow-striped bampies yours for the catching.

What happened, he thought, watching the moving tops of the far-off trees, what happened then? His skin was prickling and it was uncomfortable to lie down. It felt as though the nerve ends were very near the surface of the skin. He stirred uneasily and lay back again. The ice had melted in the glass beside the bed. He drank the liquid left but there was no taste to it, no taste at all through the furred numbness of his mouth. A car drove past. He imagined the driver, young, good-looking, a girl beside him, a blonde, surely a blonde, clean and wholesome with shaven armpits. A seaside-city girl. A poster girl. He forgot the car suddenly as the passage creaked with footsteps. They went past and a door slammed at the end of the passage.

Weekends in the summer they would cycle out to the river, three of them, and fish off someone's small sun-warped wooden jetty. The water was shallow over mud flats drilled with prawn holes, and crabs and small plump cuttle-fish lived in the thin green river weed. All those days seemed quiet and green with the tranquillity of small rivers: and in the evenings the sun went behind the red hills and the coots and cormorants and pipers whistled and hooted and the big springers started jumping and you could smell the woodsmoke from the colored fisherman's fires on the far bank.

He sat up and his head ached suddenly, throbbingly. Across the room he saw himself in the dressing-table mirror. He looked at himself without smiling.

"If I knew," he said, and watched the strange lips in the mirror move. "If I knew. But I don't know. I've never known and that's why it's like this. Nobody told me."

And then he lost interest in the river, or rather his friends did, and because friends were very important, because he didn't like doing things alone, or doing things that were not in, or with it, he stopped liking the sea and the river, and the fish and the birds too. And there were other things to be liked, too much, and he never went back to the river or the sea or the summer garden or anything like that, ever again. There was Ambition, and there was Becoming Somebody, and there was the Good Club, and there was Holding Your Liquor Like A Man; and all these were very good things: but no one ever told him that for people like him this field was mined.

"Nobody ever told me what it would be like," he said to the man in the mirror. "Nobody." Tears came out of his eyes suddenly and ran down his cheeks to the corners of his mouth and he realized that they really were salty: and then the beach with the gulls came back, and the mullet under the jetty, and the waving river grass in the clear water under the gray planking: and he knew he would go back.

He was smiling bravely at the wonderful certainty of going back when the door opened and she came in. The sun came through the window and sparkled in the brandy as she put the bottle on the table.

"Oh God," he said. "Oh God."

Behind her the sky was very blue with small white clouds coming up from the sea and the tops of the trees were waving now in the rising wind.

29

THE dark green lines of the orange-trees ran down from the house to the river. It was still early in the season and there was small green-gold fruit among the shining leaves. Beneath the trees the red earth was new-tilled and clear of weeds. Beyond the last row of trees was the river with sunlight on it and beyond the river was the high wall of the cliff.

"It's going to be a good season," said J. D. Dickason, looking at the trees.

"Looks like it," said Gord. He sat there without thinking of anything serious, watching the valley and listening to the sounds of the farmyard. The red honeysuckle below the stoep was blooming and there were bees around it. A dark blue fork-tailed drongo was sitting on the telephone wire overhead, watching the bees and the two men on the stoep. Under the gutter at one end of the stoep two martins were building a nest and the stoep was full of soft twitterings and flutterings as the birds came and went. The benches on the stoep were green-painted wrought iron, very old, prob-

[189]

ably from the garden of some big city house. The whole house was old, square, flat-roofed, with long passages and small shuttered windows and the feeling of a place which has been used by many people over many years. Gord thought it was a house he would like to live in and die in, with the martins outside his window. J. D. Dickason's grandfather had built it, he and his wife and a few Africans, in 1850, bringing big stones up from the river by ox wagon, dressing them with cold chisels. The valley had been very wild then; the Dickasons' was the first house. On the stoep now was a small brass ship's cannon; the family story was that it had been used to shoot elephants. There were still three elephant skulls, mildewed and tuskless, in the back yard, but the elephants had long since gone from the valley.

Behind the house were six big belumbra trees, forty feet high, and ten feet around the trunks, huge soft trees older than J. D. Dickason himself.

From behind them came the soft clash of plates and the smell of farm cooking: potatoes and samp and gravy and mutton and new salty butter and sour milk.

"I've never learned to eat town-style," said J. D. Dickason, sniffling. "All these bits and pieces, finicky. You need a plateful of the filling stuff. I tell you, Gord, that university's finished my Bobby. He can't eat a good meal now. He had one of his fancy girls up here a few weeks ago. Let her cook us a meal. Crayfish something-or-other. Hardly a mouthful, I promise you, with some white muck on top of it so you didn't know what you were eating. Could have been cattle lick. And when we'd finished, and Mum and I waiting for the next course, we find that that was it. Hardly enough to fill a sparrow's eye, man. Of course, I put my foot in it and said well, the sample was nice, but when do we eat, and Bobby got embarrassed and took her out with the horses, which was a good thing, because Mum and I went into the kitchen and had a real meal."

He shook his head.

"Gord, man, they don't speak our language any more. I can't hardly speak to Bobby. God knows why. And his friends. Why, man —" He stopped, looking out over the valley.

"Ah, well."

After a while he said, "The house is going, you know."

"Going?" said Gord.

"We're ripping out the insides, taking the roof off, making the windows bigger, putting a septic tank in the yard, flush sanitation inside." He laughed, briefly. "Oh, you won't recognize it in a few months' time. Got an architect from Port Elizabeth to look at it. He's going to make a genuine Cape Dutch homestead out of it."

"I thought it was," said Gord.

"Not in their language, man. It *is* the real thing, but to them the real thing is what they see in books. So they're going to make it into the real thing." He looked at the valley again. "Those oranges better come up well this year."

"It's your house," said Gord.

"It's going to be Bobby's," said J. D. Dickason. "Someday. And he'll change it then, so it might as well be done now. Says no girl will ever come and live in it as it is. Too primitive, he says. Says he's ashamed to bring his friends here."

"It's your house," said Gord.

"Yes. And he's my son."

"You're in the middle," said Gord.

"Right in the middle, Gord. Right in the middle."

"So you're giving in."

'That's right. I don't have the heart in me any more, Gord. I'm giving in. Mum and I are taking a cruise along the coast, down to Cape Town and then up to Durban and Lourenço Marques, and when we come back it'll all be done. Mum and I are going to have a little flat, like, at the back, a bedroom and our own sitting room, and Bobby can have the front."

"You're handing over the farm?"

"Gradually. I don't keep up with these modern methods, Gord. Half of those articles in the *Farmer's Weekly* I don't understand. I started farming when all you did was plow the land, turn in some manure, and pray for rain. I don't have the vocabulary to be one of these model farmers. I need a dictionary by me just to read an article in the *Farmer's Weekly* now, let alone understand it."

He tapped out his pipe on the stoep railing and the drongo flew away in fright, going in a long low sweep to the beehives beside the dairy.

"Well," he said. He sat down again and filled his pipe from a chamois tobacco bag.

"Well, I didn't bring you up here to tell you this. Thing is, Gord, the boy finishes in a few months and I've arranged a trip to Mozambique for him."

"Yes?" said Gord. "Hunting?"

"Yes. And I want you to take them up, Bobby and his friends. They can't go alone, Gord. They're useless in the bush and I'd worry about them being careless with the guns. You know what youngsters are like."

"Yes."

"I want him to see Africa, Gord. This isn't Africa any more." He waved his hand at the valley, the ordered orange-trees.

"This isn't Africa. This is something we've made. And nor is the Kruger Park Africa, nor shooting tame spring bok on somebody's farm. I want him to see the Africa you and I knew, Gord. And I want you to show it to him."

"I don't know," said Gord. "I just don't know."

"You can still shoot, Gord. You can still shoot rings around those youngsters, and walk the feet off them in the bush. You can still show them that we did know something, Gord."

"Is that what you want?" asked Gord.

J. D. Dickason sat without speaking, staring at the orange-trees moving now in the wind, and with the river beyond ruffled and sparkling.

"Yes," he said. "Yes. I think that's what I want."

Back in the hill house which seemed a long way from the freshness of the valley and the watered orange groves. The afternoon wind blowing hot and the fine sifting of sand against the house and the roof creaking and settling. Julia had opened the musty front room and wiped the dust from the two chairs and the old table and the framed photographs and the faded watercolors. There was a brown oval photograph of her grandfather in a gold frame and another of Gord's brother Stuart in his uniform, very erect and determined against a studio background of cliffs and ferns and a threading waterfall. There was a picture of her mother and father with a smug swaddled baby between them, her sister Kate, unlucky enough to be born during the Spanish influenza epidemic and not lucky enough to live through it. She looked at the picture now and tried to recall her parents, but they stared disinterestedly back at her; Father proud and rather mournful and Mother pale-faced with thin fair hair and wide set wondering eyes, Mother who was English and very proud of it, to whom England was never England but always "Home," said with a capital letter and a slight drop of the voice; she spent forty years of her life in South Africa, at Kimberly, in Bloemfontein, and in the Cape, and she lived as she would have in Yorkshire. Africa stopped at her front door and the Union Jack flew in the garden on St. George's day, Trafalgar Day, and the King's Birthday: the Afrikaners were always Boers and there was roast beef and Yorkshire pudding every Sunday, even if the tar was melting in the street outside. Father had faded away slowly over the years, resenting every minute of it, suffering all the diseases of old men, and dying one hot Saturday afternoon in the noisy public ward of the provincial hospital. Mother died like a lady, going to bed one night in her long gown and frilly nightcap and just sliding silently into death.

The watercolors were very faded now, the original penciled outlines showing through the browns and yellows and light blues. They were of Herne Bay and Las Palmas and Table Bay, and traced the immigration of some cousin of her father's. As a girl she had always liked the Las Palmas painting. It had an element of wonder and freshness, the blue sea white-streaked around the stone breakwater with the flat-fronted white buildings behind curving around the small beach and going up the brown hills. The Table Bay one was the usual stereotyped view of the beautiful mountain, the prescribed incredulity overlaying the artist's own excitement too heavily; and Herne Bay was a row of anonymous sunbathers facing a pebbled beach running down to a flat gray sea.

Now she dusted the photographs and the paintings and then sat down at the window with the bright yellow duster in her hand and looked out at the dry garden. She opened the cutlery drawer in the long table and took out her father's big Bible, bound in soft red leather, and sat with it unopened before her, deriving comfort from its presence, her fingers rubbing gently the deckled pages and feeling the grain of the good leather.

It was after dark when Gord came back. J. D. Dickason dropped him at the gate and drove on into town. Julia had lit the hanging lamp and laid the table in the front room and they ate there. The road gang was up over the hill now and from the front room they could see the red warning lights along the detour and the flicker of the fires among the corrugated-iron huts. After supper he helped her wash up and then they sat in the front room again. He was worried about telling her about J. D. Dickason but when he got it out she was quite happy. Or she seemed happy. She

[195]

sat reading the Bible with her silver-rimmed glasses low down on her nose and she was quite unworried.

"I don't like doing it, Julia," he said. "I don't like leaving you here alone. Dickason offered to have you up at the farm while I'm gone but I thought I'd ask you first."

"It's all right," she said. She smiled at him, as one would at a child.

"I won't be lonely. One need never be lonely, you know."

"It's not right," he said. "But you know that it's a good job."

"It's quite all right," she said. "I expect I'll find a lot to do with the auxiliary while you're gone."

"It's only a month," he said. "That's all."

"I'm never alone," she said. "I know I'm being looked after. I know He is watching me."

"As long as you'll be all right," he said. "I'll tell the police to watch the house."

"I don't need the police, Gord." She turned the pages of the Bible slowly, looking at him. 'Will you come to Church this Sunday?"

"Well, I — yes. Yes, I'll come," he said.

"Reverend Carey will pick us up," she said. "I'll press your suit and you can wear your good white shirt. I think a white shirt looks better than a blue one for church."

"I suppose so," said Gord. He leaned back in the chair and thought about the trip. He was not looking forward to it. He thought of Bobby Dickason and his friends. No, he was not looking forward to it.

"While you're away, perhaps I'll tell Reverend Carey he can use this room for a Bible class," said Julia. "We take it in turns and we haven't used this house yet. I thought it would be right to offer."

"Yes," he said. "Of course. I wondered why you'd cleaned out the room."

'It's not so bad, Gord, is it? It'll be all right, won't it?"

He stood up and kissed her on the forehead.

"It'll be fine, Mum. Just fine."

He went out and took down the Lee-Enfield and the Mauser automatic and laid them on the floor beside his chair while he fetched the oil and cleaning rags from his room. He only had a dozen rounds left for the Mauser and thought he might as well use them on this trip. He was trying to look forward to it.

30

A T nine o'clock in the morning it was still cool at the tables under the flame trees in the Avenida Louis Botha. They sat at two tables pulled together and drank coffee. Gord sat with Bobby Dickason and his fiancée at one table, and Harry Mulder and Theunis Nel and the other two girls sat at the next table. They had driven straight through from Johannesburg, driving all night and crossing the border as soon as it opened. The two new Ford pickups with their canvas canopies were parked across the street, which was very busy at this hour. They were covered with dust and one of them had lost a hubcap and the canopy of the other had a long tear where thieves had sliced it in Johannesburg.

He had enjoyed being in the Karroo again, even briefly: the sun was hard on the plains and the hills were a particular blue that you never saw anywhere else, at the edge of the wide olive-green and gray and red plains and in the early mornings the guinea fowl were jerkily strutting plump black shapes beneath the mimosas. The Orange Free State he had never liked and he was glad when they were through, out of the flat plateau, out of the dull city where he had last seen Edith, the memory still uncomfortable after these years, and into the Transvaal, getting into Johannesburg late at night with the streets crowded with bioscope traffic and finding a hotel near Broadcast House and leaving late the next afternoon.

Johannesburg had not been anything like he remembered it, but he was prepared for that. On the way out they had driven past the mine property where he had met Edith, but that was changed, too, with a block of tall flats standing where the tennis courts had been. He had wondered, briefly, about Edith. It was still a memory with poignancy. Then out of Johannesburg and eastwards through the Transvaal, through the good farming veld along the fast national road with smart new filling stations every few miles, down through the rolling Lebombo, the mountains still as he remembered them, down into the bushveld, through pretty Nelspruit with the flame trees in red flower over the wide streets, through Komatipoort and Ressano Garcia into Mozambique. In Ressano Garcia the customs buildings were new and the road was fresh tarred and Maricio's store was gone. Only the tall trees of the outspan still stood, and they looked unfamiliar now. They drove into Lourenço Marques in a rainstorm with the thunder growling overhead and the ships in the estuary dim shapes through the wind-blown wet; then the storm had gone out over the bay and left the town clean and fresh, the white buildings all looking new-painted when the sun came up.

The café owners put out their tables under the trees, the leaves dripping raindrops on to the starched tablecloths which would soon dry when the sun got over the housetops.

He liked being in the town again. He had always liked this town and even now, with all its changes, he still liked it. He thought the Portuguese were very wise about Africa. They went with it a little way. The places they built in Africa were not aggressively civilized. All the amenities were there, but less arrogantly than they were in South Africa or Rhodesia. This big city fitted into Africa. Johannesburg didn't. Johannesburg just was, whether Africa liked it or not. He thought Johannesburg could be transported anywhere in the world without the Johannesburgers noticing or caring very much. Johannesburg was Johannesburg and the country didn't matter very much. Lourenço Marques was not like that.

"Well," said Bobby. "Look at that, hey, look at that."

A young white man walked past with his arm around a half-caste girl.

"What do you think of that, Mr. Vance?" asked Bobby. He was superficially very polite to Gord.

Gord shrugged. "Nothing to do with us. It's their country."

"But a bloody *kaffermeid*. Man, a bloody *meid*."

"The Portugooses don't mind," said Harry Mulder. "The gooses don't mind anything."

"They know how to handle the kaffirs," said Theunis. "Man, the kaffir knows his place here."

"The gooses are half bloody kaffirs themselves," said Harry.

"They're so mixed now nobody knows who's who any more."

"Be careful," said Gord. "Most of them understand English."

He was beginning to feel embarrassed. The girls were wearing very short shorts and he was just remembering that the Portuguese were supposed to be very strict about things like that. He looked at the girls and thought again, what a farce this is.

"I want to see a bullfight while I'm here," said Bobby. "Is this the season?"

"Yes," said Gord. "It's the season all right. But they don't kill the bull here. It's just cape work."

"I saw a bullfight in Spain," said Clea. "The matador was wonderful. I've got some wonderful shots of it. He killed the bull right in front of us. Right down in front of us."

"They don't kill them here?" said Harry. "Hell, what's the point then?"

"It's all cape work," said Gord.

"I'll wait till Spain, then," said Bobby. His father was giving him a tour overseas that year. He had been talking about it for the past three days.

It was getting hotter now and the sun was coming strongly through the leaves and the fresh rain smell was going. Up the street Gord could see the beer hall and the big market building. African workers were carrying fruit and vegetables and chickens trussed together by their legs, in bunches, into the market through the big archway.

"More coffee?" asked Bobby. Gord did not hear him. He was looking along the street at the cars and the people and trying to remember what it was like forty years ago and he was slowly developing an old man's involvement with himself. Bobby touched him on the shoulder and Gord turned, slowly, not seeing him at first, still thinking of the old town, and then the others laughed and Bobby repeated the question.

"No," said Gord. "No thanks."

Bobby called the waiter and ordered coffee for the girls and beers for the men. The waiter did not speak English very well, or he did not want to, and Bobby was annoyed. He spoke shortly to the waiter:

"*Skud, kaffir*," and held up one of the empty beer bottles from another table, holding it in front of the man's face and holding up three fingers of the other hand; and then he did the same with a coffee cup. He was very offensive.

"Yes. *Obbrigado*," said the waiter, and went inside the café. His face was sullen.

"He understands, all right," said Harry. "He understands all right."

"Only one thing they understand," said Bobby. The waiter came out with the coffee and beers.

"You're a cheeky kaffir, aren't you?" asked Bobby.

"Sir?" said the waiter.

"Don't worry," said Gord to the man in Portuguese. "Don't worry about him." To Bobby he said, "I told you to be careful. These people are funny about things here. They're funny about their natives here."

"They treat them worse than we treat ours," said Bobby.

"That's true," said Harry. "I heard about it."

"I don't know about that," said Gord. "I know that's an

old South African story. But I'm telling you, they're funny about how foreigners treat the natives here."

"The Portugooses don't worry me," said Bobby.

"You're in their country," said Gord. "They'd better worry you. They can be very hard." He was tired of the argument and wished they would all go away and leave him to sit in the shade and watch the people and the cars and perhaps take a walk along the seafront or around the market.

"They love us," said Bobby. "We're their only friends. Their only rich friends."

"That's another old South African story," said Gord. He closed his mind to them again. Perhaps he would take a drive down to the fishing harbor and watch the boats come in. He wondered when the boats did come in. Probably very early in the morning after netting prawn all night, or late in the afternoon.

"Can we do something now?" asked Marie. She had not spoken since Ressano Garcia. Something had annoyed her the night before and she was not speaking to anybody.

"Can we please please do something now?" she said. "Or are we going to sit here all day?"

"All right," said Harry, relieved that she was speaking again and wishing to avoid another row, "all right, we're moving now."

"I'll fix up the licenses," said Gord. "You go'n have some fun on the beach. I'll meet you down by the Clube Navale at lunchtime."

"Well, if that's all right," said Bobby.

"I'll take the blue truck, all right? I can speak the language a little still."

"Okay," said Bobby. He gave Gord the keys.

"Don't let them *verneuk* you, Mr. Vance," said Harry Mulder. "These gooses are damn slim, man. You got to watch them."

"I'll be careful," said Gord. He stood up. He was feeling the heat and the humidity and it worried him. He had never been bothered by it before.

"By the Clube Navale," he said. He walked across the road and got into the truck. The seats were already uncomfortably hot. He wound down all the windows and unbuttoned his shirt and sat there for a few minutes, fanning himself with his hat. The truck had a small rubber-blade fan mounted on the instrument panel. He fumbled beneath the dash until he found the small toggle switch and turned it on. He opened the glove box and took out a phial of Paludrine. He shook one of the tablets onto his hand and swallowed it, wishing he had a glass of water. He had taken malaria very badly up in Tanganyika. He had not had a recurrence for ten years but he wanted to make quite sure that he did not have one on this trip. He started the engine and backed the truck carefully into the street. Across the street the three boys and their girls watched him. The trees shadowed their faces and he couldn't see whether they were smiling or laughing.

"Drive carefully," called Theunis. He was the joker. "*Ry versigtig, ou man.*" He was always careful not to be offensive.

Gord pulled out into the morning traffic and drove down

the wide street, stopping at the intersection where the traffic policeman in his white helmet surveyed the cars from his small wooden platform.

"He's a funny old man," said Clea. "The way he looks over his glasses at us."

"He's rather sweet," said Marie, "but he doesn't like us."

"Who does?" asked Bobby, and they all laughed. They watched the traffic policeman give the go-ahead and the truck drive on up the street towards the center of the city.

"Why Dad had to pick him," said Bobby. He shook his head.

"He reminds me of the Ancient Mariner," said Clea. "Tum te tum, and he stoppeth one of three."

"But why me?" asked Bobby.

"With his long gray beard and glittering eye," said Theunis.

"But he hasn't got a beard," said Marie. She was becoming quite pleasant again.

"He has a glittering eye," said Clea.

"Peering through bifocals," said Theunis.

"You're horrible," said Freddie, pulling a face at Theunis so he knew she did not really mean it. Her full name was Frederika but only her grandmother called her that. She was a thin girl with a large nose and slightly protruding eyes and when she wanted to she could be very coarse indeed, something which would have surprised her grandmother.

"Well, are we going?" said Marie. They called the Indian waiter and paid the bill. Theunis and Freddie and Harry got in the back of the pickup and Bobby and Clea sat up in the cab. They drove down to the Cardoso Hotel and booked a three-bed room for the boys and a double and a single room for the girls. This was to be a very proper safari.

Gord drove slowly through the town. He changed some money at a bank in the Avenida Republica and then arranged the hunting licenses. Afterwards he drove past the old hospital, which looked very much as it had forty years ago, except that there was a new surgical block with some very expensive Chevrolet ambulances parked outside. Behind the low red roofs of the old hospital a new hospital was being built, five stories high, of white stone which hurt the eyes in the sunlight. On the front façade of the building there was a larger-than-life bas-relief of some religious subject which Gord did not recognize. He went past without stopping and took the street down to the beach. Along the road to the Clube Navale the grass was very green and fresh and the flame trees were bright with new flowers. The beach was very crowded and the camping site with its gray sand was packed with brown and white tents and caravans and cars and trucks from South Africa and Rhodesia. Some of them were from other parts of Mozambique but mostly they were from South Africa and Rhodesia.

In between the caravans Africans in khaki smocks were raking the sand with wide rakes. Along the beach below the camping grounds there were cafés selling fruit and ice cream and Coca-Cola. Across the wide calm bay he could see the low blue shadow of Inhaca Island. There were three freighters anchored out in the channel. The nearest was a green-and-gray Safmarine ship. She was empty and riding very high and red lead patches were bright below the Plimsoll line. He guessed she was waiting for a berth in the harbor. Far out in the bay was a small yacht.

He parked the car below the white Polana Hotel with its turquoise swimming bath and beautiful garden and walked slowly along the beach until he found Bobby and his friends. The sand was deep and soft and when he found them beneath a striped umbrella he was sweating and his glasses had misted. He sat down beside Bobby.

"It's all fixed," he said.

"Good," said Bobby. "We're booked in at the Cardoso. Thought we might as well stay the night."

"I want a bed tonight," said Marie. "I don't want another night like last night. That damn truck."

"All right," said Gord. "We should get out early tomorrow, though."

"We going to eat?" asked Harry.

"I am," said Gord.

"I'll lie a bit," said Bobby. He was gleaming with olive oil.

"Watch this sun," said Gord. He stood up and the beach and sea swam, briefly around him. He wanted to get inside, out of the sun, out of the glare. His skin had lost the elasticity of youth and now he could feel the sun driving hard on it, stretching it taut across his face and the backs of his hands, his knees, his shoulders through his shirt. He was wearing clip-on sunshields over his glasses but the glare still hurt him and he was getting a headache from the strain of keeping his eyes screwed up.

[207]

"Here's your key," said Bobby. He felt around in the pocket of his shirt and gave Gord a small key on a plastic tag. "You know where the Cardoso is?"

"Yes," said Gord. "I'll see you there."

"Right," said Bobby. "Cheerio, then." The others lay with their shining backs to the sun, faces pillowed on their arms. They had not looked up. Gord walked back through the heavy sand to the road. He sat in the cab with the fan blowing on his face. After a while he drove down the beach road past the Clube and up around the Polana. As he passed he saw the six brown backs beneath the big bright umbrella.

"You're a fool," he said. "A bloody old fool, and nothing's worse than that."

Back in the hotel he pulled the curtains and took off his clothes and lay in the cool dark listening to the children splashing in the pool outside. He wanted to go to sleep but he could not. He lay on the edge of sleep all afternoon and at five he got up and had a shower and put on a clean shirt and slacks and went through to the empty bar and had a cold beer, drinking it very slowly and watching the tree-shaded street outside. He was feeling very depressed, the depression that comes from sleeping badly on a hot afternoon; and something else besides.

31

THEY left early the next day, getting clear of Lourenço Marques before sunup. The road was good for ten miles and then the bitumen ended and the red dirt was badly corrugated so that the trucks with their heavy duty springs bounced very uncomfortably. It was very dry away from the coast and the dust came into the cabs, chokingly, and covered everything with a thin film. Everybody was very bad-tempered, and breakfast, fifty miles out, was eaten in silence. Gord watched the girls and saw that they weren't enjoying it at all.

You wanted to come, he thought. You wanted to go on safari. You've seen all those safari bioscopes and you wanted to come. Now you're finding out what it's like. Hot and dirty and flies in your food and everything tasting of paraffin after a few days and lukewarm water and no milk and sunburn and heat exhaustion and all that pretty eye makeup dissolving as you sweat, and those fancy hair-dos that cost you so much in Johannesburg just frizzing away in the sun and dust. He finished his eggs and bacon and wiped the plate clean with a piece of bread. Now that they were out in the bush he felt a little better, but he was still sweating a lot and his eyes still hurt. He was worried about shooting with the bifocals, and he was worried about them misting up so much. He had a small piece of chamois leather in his pocket and he kept wiping them but it didn't help much.

I shouldn't have come on this, he thought, looking at the young people. I'm past all this now. But I thought it would be good, I really did, and I wanted to see the proper bush again. I'm tired of plowed fields and planted forests and game parks. And I need the money. Most of all I need the money, and this is the only way I can get it. Or I can go into an old folks' home, Julia and me, or I can throw myself on the mercy of some town council and get a job as a weed picker in the public gardens, or an attendant in the midtown public lavatories. Well, you should have thought of all this thirty years ago, he told himself, sternly, you should have thought of it then. But everything was fun then and the future always seemed a long way off and besides it was then, in his circle, the thing to laugh at talk of security or "prospects" or pensions.

He wiped his knife and fork with a twist of newspaper and put them and his plate in the box bolted to the floor of the blue pickup. He took a long drink out of the water bag and he was ready to go. He watched the others clean their plates and put them away. When they had packed and got back into the trucks Gord walked back and buried a baked bean tin and an egg carton and ground out a cigarette stub which was smoldering in the long grass.

They watched him through the windshield without speaking, Bobby shaking his head. Gord got into the truck finally and they pulled out onto the road, the second truck riding five hundred yards behind the first to avoid its dust.

"You think we're messy campers, Mr. Vance?" said Bobby after a few miles. He had been thinking about it and now he was angry and there was an ugly sound to his voice.

"No," said Gord. "It's just a habit of mine, cleaning up. And that *stompie* could have started a fire. Bush's pretty dry around here."

Bobby clamped his jaw and stared ahead through the dusty windshield. After a while he switched on the radio and juggled the tuning until he picked up Lourenço Marques radio loud and clear. They drove through the sunlit dusty afternoon with a record request program rattling the loudspeaker.

They camped for the night on a piece of high ground with big rocks scattered among the thorn. It was very quiet up here and "Shenandoah" was coming over the radio. Gord sat with his back against the truck and listened to the soft lovely music going out over the dark bush and thought of the big ships going down the Atlantic. That was another thing he would have liked. Then he thought of England and of his father, especially of his father, and he remembered the faded red coat and the white helmet which used to hang in the cupboard behind the front door, the braid greening through the years, the moths gradually riddling the good doeskin; and the old lever-action single-shot Snider rifle in the gun rack, such a slow gun that when you shot target on the hill across from the house you could jack another bullet into the chamber before the first one raised dust at two hundred yards. Yet they had been good stopping guns, as Cetewayo had found out.

In the thick forests along the Uganda–Belgian Congo border they were followed all day and all night by the pygmies. They were always there, but never seen, and the Kikuyu guides were terrified and kept very close to the white men; one day Gord shot an unknown antelope along a small stream and left it for the pygmies. When they passed that way the next day, going back to the main camp, the animal was gone, and there were small footprints all around the place where they had left it.

He sat beside the truck and watched the light go over the bush and listened to the radio without resentment now, because it had given him "Shenandoah." After they had eaten he had a small brandy and went to bed early. He did not feel like talking and in any case he found that their talk was hard for him to understand, full of private jokes and hidden meanings which left him feeling clumsy and stupid. He lay awake again for a long while, listening to the talking and the hard laughter, and later a wind came up from the south, moving the branches and pattering gravel against the truck. He pulled the blanket over his head and went to sleep with the sound of the windy bush all around him and when he awoke it was just dawn and very still again and there was fine white mist in the valley below the hill with the tops of the trees standing out of it like islands in a flood.

They shot a few crocodiles along a little tributary of the Limpopo and a pair of good waterbuck, one of them with really wide horns, and Gord began to enjoy himself. The waterbuck were shot well in difficult country, by Gord and Bobby, after Harry and Theunis had missed. They had kept the horns and given the meat to a native kraal a few miles upstream. The country here was still very wild with plenty of small game and birds along the river. In the reeds there were big colonies of black-and-yellow weaver birds, and sometimes the plump red-and-black bishop birds.

Gord had brought his old opera glasses with him and he spent whole afternoons watching the weaver birds and the coots in the reeds and the herons standing still and gray in the muddy water. He was quite content to look now. He had only shot the waterbuck on an impulse, because it was far and going fast through low bush and he had felt just then that it would quite probably be the last good shot he would ever make at a running buck. It had been almost a snap shot and the back sight was just beginning to blur when he squeezed off.

He walked back to camp this afternoon and when he was a hundred yards away he could hear Lourenço Marques radio Record Club coming over the radio very loud. When he came through the last bush Bobby and Clea were jiving around the truck, their feet raising the loose dust. There was a small pile of beer bottles at the tailgate of the green pickup and he could smell brandy.

Gord put the Lee-Enfield in the back of the truck and walked around to the cab and turned the radio off. Bobby and Clea stopped dancing and looked at him.

"I could hear that right down at the river," he said. "Guess everything in miles heard it."

"So?" said Bobby. He had been drinking warm beer in the sun all afternoon and now he was irritably drunk.

"I thought we were going along the river tonight," said Gord.

"To hell with that," said Bobby. "We're having a party."

"Have a drink, Mr. Vance," said Harry.

"Have a drink, big white hunter," said Theunis.

"No," said Gord. He had a long drink of water from the canvas cooler. From the trees behind the trucks two buck, a duiker and a reedbuck, were hanging. The duiker was a young ewe. They had been gutted and now hung stiff, tongues and eyes protruding, twisting slowly in the afternoon wind.

Gord leaned against the truck and looked at the dead buck, the flies shining on them.

To this, he thought. I must come back to this. And I thought it would be so good. He sat on the tailgate and listened to the bush. Now that the radio was off the birds and insects were calling again.

He sat on the tailgate and looked at the young people. Bobby was slightly unsteady on his feet now. He was sweating a lot and his fleshy face with its blue stubble was ugly and old. Theunis and Harry were sitting on the ground with beer cans held half-ashamedly between their knees. Clea was brushing her hair, using the truck's rear-view mirror. Marie and Freddie were lying on a blanket, reading magazines. They had long since become bored with the whole thing and passed the days listening to the radio or reading. Now Freddie rolled over and made a face.

"Why's the radio off?" she said. "I want music."

"Father says we're making a noise," said Bobby, sneering.

"Oh, the meanie," said Freddie. Her mouth smiled at him.

"Please can I have it on?"

"You can do what you like," said Gord. He stood up and picked up the rifle. He went around the cab and switched on the radio. Jazz erupted into the bush.

He walked slowly out of the camp. Behind the green pickup the three Africans were sitting around a small fire, wrapped in their blankets. They greeted him softly as he went past. He stopped and they looked at him impassively.

"Did Senhor Bobby give you food tonight?" Gord asked. The eldest shook his head.

"Come," said Gord. He went back into camp, the African following him. He took bread and margarine out of the truck and some coffee and sugar. Bobby and the others watched him without speaking. The radio was still blaring. Gord cut the duiker down and said to the African "Take that," and the old man picked it up, slinging it over his shoulder.

Bobby came up and stood in front of Gord.

"What're you giving the kaffir my buck for?" he asked.

"He's got to eat," said Gord. "Even kaffirs've got to eat,

you know. They haven't filled up on booze all day. They're hungry."

"You take a lot on yourself," said Bobby.

"That's all right," said Gord.

"You take a lot on yourself for a hired hand," said Bobby.

"That's all right, Bobby," said Gord. He was trying very hard to keep his temper. He said to the African in Portugese, "Go on with it," and the old man walked around and dropped the buck in front of the other two behind the pickup.

"You don't want to be out of a job, do you?" said Bobby. "You don't want that, do you? You're going the right way about it. You're certainly going the right way about it."

"Your father hired me," said Gord. He felt himself flushing. "But we can call it off anytime, Bobby." He turned and walked through the camp and along the game path to the river. It was now late afternoon and the muddy water was very smooth and almost blue under the bright evening sky. He heard pheasants calling in the thick bush along the far bank. Gord sat in an open stretch of bank and watched the sun go down. As the bush grew quieter he could hear the radio again and sometimes, on an eddy of wind, a girl laughing.

To hell with them, he thought. This was a mistake. But I'm glad I didn't lose my temper today. That Bobby is a nasty job all round and especially when he's drunk. He would have hit me this afternoon, he would have hit me without a doubt, and I just couldn't handle him now. Twenty years ago he wouldn't have been a breakfast for me, but not now. He sat looking at the water and enjoying the quiet of the darkening bush.

It grew cold when the sun was down and the night wind stirred the bush and slapped the water against the bank. The sky was very clear, still yellow in the west, and the stars were bright and big.

He walked slowly back to camp, treading carefully in the dark, because he was afraid of puff adders lying on the still-warm path, and when he came back to the trucks Bobby and his friends had gone to sleep around the fire and the radio was hissing faintly. He switched off the radio and groped around until he found a blanket and then curled up beneath the green pickup. During the night he awoke and heard voices above him and a soft shuffling and then the truck began to creak rhythmically on its springs. After that he lay awake for a long while, listening to the bush and watching the Africans sitting around the small red glow of their fire, wondering what they thought about all this; and finally, before he fell asleep again, he thought of Julia. He had never really resigned himself to Julia and now he felt guilty.

The next morning everybody was rather sorry about the night before and feeling their hangovers very badly in the heat and dust. They broke camp after lunch and by the time they had packed the trucks and got back on the road to Tete it was four o'clock. Gord had been impatient at the delay but he let things ride and by sundown Bobby was almost friendly again. Perhaps I'll last, thought Gord, watching him, perhaps I'll last out after all. Only another four days and I've done it. He had not taken the money in advance, only twenty pounds for his expenses, because he had doubted his ability to tolerate Bobby and his friends for two weeks; but now he had almost done it and when he got back the money would be waiting for him in his account at Barclays Bank. It was going to make a lot of difference. He leaned back on the hot seat and thought about it. A hundred pounds less the twenty advance. If only he had had a break like this before the Ford went wrong. If only he had had a couple of breaks like this a few years ago. But he couldn't have done it a few years ago. He was independent then and *hardegat* and people did it his way or not at all. Now he wasn't like that at all. He thought of the night before and smiled faintly. Now he wasn't like that at all.

He looked at the .22 Savage on the seat between them and thought, I wouldn't have done this before. Except the waterbuck and the crocodiles, they had shot everything from the trucks: reedbuck, the duiker ewe, a wildebeest. The wildebeest they had chased across the open veld outside Vila Fontes, almost running it down, Harry shooting it finally from twenty yards as it stood gasping. Gord had stopped protesting after the first day when it was made very clear to him that he could shut up or get out. He could not afford to get out so he shut up and hated it in silence. Now Bobby had taken to driving with the Savage beside him. It was a beautiful, good gun, with a huge charge driving the little bullet, but Gord didn't think it was the gun to use against heavy game. He had no faith in the stopping power of the light bullet.

"You don't know about these modern guns," said Bobby. "It's got the speed man, God knows how many thousand feet a second. It'll drop anything."

"It hasn't got the impact," said Gord. "That little bullet. A big bullet going slow's got stopping power. That little slug'll go right through a buffalo without hurting him, anyway without hurting him quick enough."

"You'll see," said Bobby.

"Stick with us, Mr. Vance," said Theunis. "We'll make you famous."

"Or dead," said Harry, and they all laughed.

Think of the money, Gord told himself. Think of the money, and shut up. He sat back and thought about Evelyn and the lions and the young adjutant on the Rufiji and the old sergeant major at Spion Kop and Stuart and the rooikat and all the other good times and when he closed his ears and his eyes and sat there with the sun on his face he could almost believe this was a good time too; but then something would intrude and he knew that not only was this a very bad time but it was going to be his last time, because he could never enjoy the bush again after this. He just wanted to get this trip over. He did not know what he would do after this, but all he wanted now was to get it over. He had expected it to be as bad as the time Hammersley and his lawyer friend shot the bushbuck, but it was worse, far worse. It was worse than he had thought possible. He dozed.

He was on Kilimanjaro again, he and Evelyn climbing up alone, and a wind blowing the snow from the peaks

[219]

*over them, and the rocks black where the wind had
scoured away the snow. The wind was very cold but the air
was exhilarating and when they turned and looked back
they could see all Africa beneath them, stretching away
green and brown and river-wrinkled through the blowing
snow.*

He awoke with a jerk, and the radio was loud and crackling, the volume rising and falling as the truck wound
through the low hills. The sun was low down and the
dust lay over the road like sea mist along the coast after
a big sea, the sun coming yellow through it. They were
driving too fast along the narrow rutted road with its high
sump-scraping *middelmannetjie* when the big leopard ran
across in front of them. Gord had time to wonder even
then, in that startled second, what made a leopard run
across the open road in front of a noisy truck, in broad
daylight: and then Bobby swore and braked and the pickup was sliding sideways and Bobby was firing the Savage
under the raised windshield, the shots very loud, the echoes
clanging on the bare metal roof and the cordite smell very
strong on the thick hot air: *bwoww! bwoww!* Two shots
with the leopard, frightened now and running low almost
lost in the bush: and then Gord saw the flash of yellow
and black through the grass as the cat rolled, kicking,
before recovering and going with a rush through the thin
line of scrub fringing the road.

Bobby closed the breech of the Savage and clicked the
safety on. Gord sat there with the Lee-Enfield up between
his knees, furiously angry and afraid of speaking yet.

"I hit him!" shouted Bobby. "I hit him, okay. Did you see that? By Jesus, I hit him, okay."

The truck's engine was still running and Bobby switched it off, impatiently. The dust they had raised settled on the bush. They had been a little ahead of the other truck and now it arrived, skidding with the wheels locked, and Harry and the girls got out.

"Did you see him?" asked Bobby. "Man, did you see him?"

"What was it?" asked Clea. "A lion?"

"A lion!" said Freddie, impressed.

"A leopard," said Theunis.

"A leopard," said Bobby, shortly. He had a lot of confidence now and he was wishing it had been a lion.

"I hit him, hey, Mr. Vance? I hit him with my last one."

"You winged him," said Gord, looking at the bush. "Now we've got to find him."

"He's probably dropped," said Bobby. "He's probably down behind the bush. Man, did you see him roll? I got him, okay."

"How would you know?" said Gord. "How the hell would you know?"

They stopped talking and laughing and looked at him.

"I hit him," said Bobby. "You saw him go."

"You hit him," said Theunis. "Hell, you hit him all right."

"With this," said Bobby, patting the Savage. "With this little baby, man."

"All right," said Gord. "You hit him. Now which one of you's going to finish him?"

"Hell, he's probably just up there, dead," said Bobby.

"All right," said Gord. "You go get him."

He sat on the running board and watched while Harry and Theunis fetched their guns and joined Bobby going carefully through the bush. He wasn't worried about the leopard jumping through the bush. He wasn't worried about the leopard jumping them there. He knew it would have gone further than that. They went carefully up to the top of the road ridge and looked back and waved.

"So," said Gord, smiling. He stood up and slid a round into the chamber of the rifle and walked up the slope to Bobby. Here the grass was broken and bloodied just a little but not enough to make it immediately important.

"How's it look?" asked Bobby. His confidence had all gone now and here in the bush with blood on the grass he was nervous.

"What do you think?" said Gord. "What the hell do you think? I told you not to use that on anything bigger than a duiker."

"What's next?" said Bobby, trying to smile. He turned quickly and walked back to the trucks. The pickup he had skidded was half off the road. Bobby went around to the back and reached in over the tailgate and took out a beer. He jerked off the cap against the bumper and the beer fountained yellow and white over his shirt.

"We'll give him a chance to peg," he said to Gord. He drank the beer and opened another bottle. It was very quiet here. There were bees around the prickly pear and bright butterflies low in the long grass.

Gord checked the magazine in the Lee-Enfield. He knew he was going to have to finish this and he wanted to do it very quickly. He was worried about his eyes. He had lost all confidence in them for this sort of shooting but he tried not to think about it.

Harry and Theunis came back down the slope and opened beers. They stood at the back of the truck and drank them. The beers were warm and frothy.

"I think he was hit bad," said Theunis.

"How would you know?" asked Gord.

"No need to get like that, Dad," said Harry, and the girls laughed.

"He's cross with us," said Theunis. "Aren't you, my old Dad?"

"You like to go in, sonny boy?" said Gord, smiling without any humor at all. He held the rifle out to Theunis.

"You like to go in and get him?"

And then it was suddenly very quiet and Theunis wasn't smiling any more, just looking at Gord over his beer with his face very red.

"You're trying your luck, old man," he said. "You're trying your luck."

"You try me," said Gord. "You just try me."

"Okay," said Bobby. "Okay okay okay for chrissake. Let's just go'n finish it, hey?"

He was sweating and a little drunk from drinking three beers quickly in the heat.

There was foam around his mouth and his shirt was limp with beer and sweat. He picked up the Savage.

"I'd take the Mauser," said Gord. He was still trying.

"I'll take this," said Bobby. He was being very stubborn
now. The beers had put something back into him. The girls
had got back into the cab of the blue pickup to get out of
the sun and they were watching him and in the shadowed
back of the green pickup, under the dusty canopy, the eyes
of the Africans were very wide and white. Poor bastards,
thought Gord. They know what's coming. He looked at
Bobby and the Savage. What the hell, he thought. I'll be
doing the shooting, anyway. His glasses had misted again
and he took them off and wiped them carefully and felt
the first tremor of fear shiver treacherously through him,
like a cold breath over his hot skin. Well, he thought, and
that's the first time, too, and at this late stage. The Africans got out of the pickup and Gord cocked the Lee-Enfield and took the safe off and he and Bobby walked slowly
through the grass with the Africans behind them. They got
to where the grass and low brush thinned out very quickly
to a short plain below, falling away to the river, with big
loose stones and red antheaps and aloe bushes. There was
dark blood on the grass and a smear on a stone. Seventy
yards away was a clump of thorn, with prickly pear growing in it, all tangled together. He heard the trucks grinding
noisily up the slope behind him, bulldozing the grass and
bush. Bobby looked at the bloodied grass and the thorn
clump.

"Think he's hit bad?" he asked, hopefully.

"Not bad enough," said Gord, watching the thorn. The
trucks were making a lot of noise.

"Can't the kaffirs beat him out?" asked Bobby.

"You tell them to," said Gord, smiling. "You're the boss." He was feeling better now. This was his ground again.

Bobby spoke to the Africans in English and Xhosa and Afrikaans.

The eldest African listened politely and when Bobby was finished he shook his head.

"*Haikona, Baas,*" he said. He had worked on the Johannesburg mines and he spoke English and Afrikaans and Xhosa and some Zulu and Sotho and Portuguese.

"*Haikona, Baas,*" he said again, and shook his head, this time with decision. He had come back from Johannesburg with some capital and now he could decline to go into any bush for any wounded leopard, for this baas or any other.

"You cheeky bloody kaffir," said Bobby, getting vicious with fear and humiliation at his fear.

"Yes, *Baas,*" said the African, smiling. He was not at all offended.

"That'll do," said Gord, quietly, and he and the Africans started down towards the thicket of thorn and pear: he did not look back to see if Bobby was with them. They found more blood on the grass lower down and they went wide around the thicket without being able to see anything in it. The sunlight coming through the branches was broken and diffused and Gord knew he would never be able to see the leopard unless it moved. They were half way around the thicket when he heard one of the trucks start and when they came around the last clump of jutting pear they saw it was over the ridge, bumping down the slope between the big stones and antheaps. Harry was driving with Clea and Freddie in the cab and Bobby was hanging onto the running board with one arm hooked inside the cab. Then the second pickup came over the ridge, whining in extra low, and Theunis took it down the slope and around the back of the thicket. The dust came up on the rising wind and blew across the bush. Gord stood and watched the trucks.

"All right," he said, slowly, seeing the way it was to be. "All right."

He spoke to the old African in Portuguese: "Go round with the trucks, you and your people," he said. "That man will frighten the leopard out with the truck. You keep behind the truck and the leopard will not worry about you."

The Africans looked at him, not liking it any more than he did, but the eldest one said *"Obbrigado"* with real feeling and they went, coming up to the thicket behind the swaying blue truck like infantry advancing behind a tank.

Gord looked at the thicket and moved sideways to get an aloe out of his line of fire. His eyelids were fluttering and his eyes kept watering and his glasses were misting again. He pushed them up on his forehead and closed his eyes against the glare for a few seconds. Then he put them back on and lifted the Lee-Enfield and sighted along the barrel and the front sight wavered and blurred after a second, as though seen through water. I'll have to shoot damn well and damn quick, he thought. I'm only going to get one shot. But now I'm not frightened, not like I was back there. My eyes must give me a second, that's all. He lowered the rifle and squeezed his eyes closed again. Red lights flickered across his closed lids.

Then he opened his eyes and turned, looking back for the other truck, and he saw that Bobby had got into the cab and screwed up the passenger-side windshield for shooting. The Savage was poking out from under the dusty windshield. He walked back to the truck and pulled open the door on Bobby's side.

"Get out," he said. "For God's sake. You don't do it like that. You wanted to shoot. Now do it the way it should be done, for God's sake."

"It'll be all right from here," said Bobby, watching the bush and not looking at Gord. "It'll be all right from here."

The girls and Harry were silent and nervous beside him, looking out under the windshield.

"You get out," said Gord. He looked back, quickly: the truck was near the thicket, almost on it. "My *Here*," he said, "but your father'll hear about this."

"Leave him alone," said Clea. Her mouth was pulled down and Gord saw she was very frightened suddenly. "Can't you leave him alone?"

"It'll be all right from here," said Bobby. "Only a bloody leopard, man. It'll be all right." He looked at the bush and fingered the bolt of the Savage.

"You little bastard," said Gord. He turned away and then he heard the truck creak as Bobby got out. Bobby caught up with him and they went down the slope together.

"I'll remember this, Mr. Vance," he said.

"Just watch the bush," said Gord. "That's all you've got

to do. Don't worry about anything. I'll get him if you don't. Have you got your sights down?"

"You shut up," said Bobby, "you just shut up." His voice was up and down the scale and his hands were shaking. The blue pickup was out of sight behind the thicket now, the engine roaring and the gearbox whining: then the V–8 died to a low bubbling and the horn sounded so suddenly and loudly, a wild brazen blare through the bush, that they both jumped. Then the leopard was out of the bush forty yards away, quite silently and terribly fast, not slowed at all yet by the .22 solid bullet which had punched through its lower ribs; skidding and making a confused half-turn at first, its eyes adjusting from shadow to sun, and then it was coming at the men in long runs and bounds through the yellow grass, snake-like: the Savage made a high sharp spitting crack and Gord heard the frantic metallic lashing of the bolt beside him as the bullet flailed the grass and whined off a rock. The leopard was big over his front sight and he stood solid, feeling himself in with his feet, the rifle snug across his chest and the solid thrusting against his shoulder and the other thud right with it, two sounds together, like the echo from the walls of a storm-water tunnel they used to shout up as kids: *bwammm . . . whap!* and the leopard skidding, tail twitching, fine eyes angry still, the beautiful head lovely no more, and new blood shocking on the grass, redder than he ever remembered it. He put the safety on and looked back at the truck, jammed against an antheap with Bobby sliding quickly down from the bonnet where he had jumped after that first shot, throwing the Savage wildly into the bush. Gord picked up the new rifle and closed the breech and walked to the truck and gave it to Bobby. With some final compassion he said:

"Told you to put your sights down."

32

AND now it was late afternoon with the sun low across the bush and the shadows dark beneath the thorn trees. The breeze was cool and smelling of mimosa flowers and cactus flowers and there was the promise of rain in it. They sat in the folding canvas chairs around the camp table which they had not used before and drank gin and tonic, the gin warm, the tonic warm and fizzy, and the lemon rather shriveled, and everyone was very complimentary about Gord. He tried to shrug it off but it was no good and finally he let it go. He felt sorry for Bobby now and he wished they would drop the subject but they kept coming back to it, over and over and over. The boys had skinned the leopard and the beautiful yellow-and-black skin, ears, tail and all, was tacked to a sapling framework leaning against the truck. There were powder marks and flash burns on the fur between the ears. The Africans were sitting around their fire beyond the trucks and talking quietly among themselves.

Whenever Gord looked up one of them was looking at

him or Bobby. Gord had two gins, drinking them very slowly. The spirits made him feel a little better but he was still very tired and yet he knew he would not be able to sleep. He watched the sun go down towards the blue Lebombo and he knew he would not be able to sleep.

"Here's to our white hunter," said Clea, lifting her glass. She had drunk four or five strong gins and they were showing.

"To our white hunter," said Freddie, chewing on a lemon rind and opening her eyes very wide.

"Please," said Gord.

"My father always told me you were good," said Bobby. He was trying to take it very well. Earlier he had tried to say that the Savage had jammed but that had been received with polite silence and some embarrassed looks, so he had dropped that now and was trying to regain face by being very frank and self-deprecatory about the whole thing. "I'm just not cut out for the safari life," he said.

"Not everybody is," said Gord, wishing he would shut up.

"They used to call you 'The Man with the Eagle Eyes,' up in Tanganyika, didn't they?" said Bobby. He wanted everyone to see how grateful he was to Gord and that he didn't feel at all bad about anything.

"That was my cousin," said Gord.

"I thought it was you."

"No."

"Can't we forget it?" said Marie. She was bored with it all. "I'm sure Mr. Vance has heard enough about it."

"Yes, yes," said Gord. "For Heaven's sake let's forget it."

"Bobby won't forget it, will you, Bobby?" said Clea, smiling beautifully.

"I'm taking a walk along the river," said Gord. "Gin's too much for me."

He walked across the dry and tufty grass to the pickup and dropped the tailgate and got inside. He opened his suitcase and felt under his shirts and spare trousers until he found the big Mauser automatic. He put it in the pocket of his bush jacket and got out of the truck, leaving the tailgate hanging down. He went down the slope past the Africans around their fire and through the screen of thorn trees to the game path along the river. The sun was almost down now and in the shadowed valley the nightjars were calling and already there were bats among the trees, and in the bushes there were the soft stirrings of night insects.

The river was flat and smooth, bright in the last night, the mud along the edge shining.

He walked carefully along the edge, smelling the coming night and feeling the nearness of the bush and thought that the next morning would be beautiful. Along the river a way was a wide grassy bank with a big tree whose name he did not know leaning out over the river. He sat with his back to the tree and watched the river sliding silently past. He was very happy now with the happiness that comes from making a long-deferred decision. He took the Mauser out of his pocket and worked the action slowly, watching the big, dull-gleaming brass cartridge come up out of the magazine and slide into the chamber. He laid the automatic carefully on the stiff grass beside him.

He sat there very silently and thought about a lot of things. He thought about the town and felt the bitterness well up inside him so he forced himself to think of other things, of Evelyn and Stuart and snow on the high mountains and wind down on the plains, blowing cold through the gray thorn and dust clouds on the desert and the first taste of water after a bad day and the feel of a new laundered shirt and the sight of duck flying at sunset.

So, well, he thought, smiling, so it hasn't been so bad and you have nothing to be really bitter about, not compared with what happened to other people, have you? You never had it really hard. You had bad times, but then so did everybody, in the depression. You never went on the dole or the road gangs and you never starved and you were never humiliated, and others were. Fred Tinsdale, with his big job in the wool company: he was a buyer with a company car and expenses, but when the depression came and wool prices fell he went on the road with the municipal pick gangs. It broke his heart and for all those years he worked in the streets with his dirty hat pulled low and his head down between his shoulders, frightened that some friend from the old days would see him: but all his friends from the old days were doing the same thing and nobody ever saw him; but the shame stayed, and even afterwards, when he had a good job again, he never lifted his head. He passed the rest of his life in constant terror of losing his job and his pension. Well, I was never like Fred, thought Gord. I was lucky. Thinking of it now this way was strange. He had always thought of Fred as the lucky one, with his good job and his pension and his family and house and car. He had forgotten the depression. That was Fred's war wound.

In those days he was at Ford. They were good people. He worked right through the depression: sometimes only three days a week, but at least he worked. Every morning at seven there would be a crowd of men walking up the empty early-morning street towards the plant, their eyes on the powerhouse smokestack: if it was smoking, it meant the power plant was getting up steam and there would be work for some men that day. But you never crawled, he thought, remembering it now with pleasure, you never crawled, even at the gate, with the men jostling to catch the foreman's eye, you never crawled, you just stood tall and somehow you were always picked.

He had sat silent and unmoving for so long that a flock of wood pigeons came in high across the river and landed in the big tree above him, fluttering and cooing as they settled in for the night. The river was dark as molten metal now and in the west the last sun was yellow on the first summer grass in the high Lebombo. He picked up the Mauser, feeling the old pleasure at the heft of a good gun and smelling the cordite and gun oil and feeling the worn wood butt solid in his palm and he remembered Stuart and the Colt and the buck across the kloof and in the evening dimness beneath the tree he smiled at the thought of that good shot. He rested the Mauser on his knee and took off the safety catch.

"You always were a lucky son-of-a-gun," he said to the river.

They had watched him go, sitting silent and awkward around the table with the sun winking on the gin bottle and the empty glasses. When he was gone through the trees Marie sighed noisily, puffing out her cheeks.

"Well, thank God," she said. Clea was looking at the bush and the path Gord had taken.

"He's quite a character," said Clea, who was taking a course in sociology or something like that, and thought of herself as an objective and yet very analytical observer of the social scene. "He's an interesting social phenonomen," she said, holding out her glass. "A little one, Bobby darling. Yes, he's a very interesting phenonomen. A uniquely *African* social phenonomen,"

"Oh, please," said Marie.

"But he *is*," said Clea, sitting up very straight and getting her serious look.

"He's the typical 'old Africa hand' of the boys' adventure books, and now things have changed all around him, and he resents it, and refuses to adapt, to evolve . . . he's lost the ability to adapt, to *evolve* . . ."

"He resents it all right," said Bobby.

"I meant *please* let's not go on about him any more," said Marie. "I'm sick to death of it."

"No, he's stood still," said Clea. "You could probably find his parallel in the hillbillies of the American Ozarks."

"Oh, hang, he's hardly a hillbilly," said Theunis.

"Well, perhaps that's not a good analogy," said Clea. "But the underlying cause is the same, this resentment of innovation, this stubborn refusal to *evolve*. You have to evolve or go under."

"Like the dinosaurs," said Theunis, laughing.

"Well, that's a fair analogy," said Clea. "Except that in their case the evolution required was primarily a physical one, and in our friend's case it's a mental one."

"Oh, for God's sake," said Marie. "I'm going to bed."

"No, *do* let's listen to Clea," said Freddie. "I like it when she gets all intellectual. It makes me so ashamed of my little B.A."

"You *can* be bitchy, Freddie," said Clea, sidetracked for a moment. She fished the lemon rind out of her glass and nibbled it daintily.

"You see, in his time and place, in his *era*, he was quite probably *perfectly* adapted and probably quite indispensable, in his time and place," said Clea. She found the anomaly of Gord's existence quite fascinating. She was thinking that she could get a good thesis out of it.

"He was quite indispensable today," said Harry, smiling at Bobby.

"All right, all right," said Bobby.

"Oh, Harry," said Freddie.

Clea poured herself another drink and sat watching the sunset. She was thinking of a title for her thesis.

Three hundred yards away, on the bank of the sunset river, Clea's social phenomenon put the wide cool muzzle of the Mauser snug under his right ear and pulled the trigger quickly and nervously, as though frightened he would change his mind; the wood pigeons startled out of the tree with a wild racketing of wings, going high and lost in the darkening sky.

GLOSSARY

Baas. master, equivalent of the East African "bwana"

Bampies. small silver fish with yellow longitudinal stripes

Bilharzia snail. small brown snail found throughout Africa and the Orient; host animal to the Bilharzia worm which causes the painful Bilharzia [redwater] disease

Bilbtong. jerked meat

Bobbejane. baboons

Boerbul. large, crossbred dog

Braaivleis. barbecue

Cerveja. beer (Portuguese)

Dassie. rock rabbit; small animal like a guinea pig

Disselboom. wagon tongue

Donga. gully

Donner. strike, hit

Dorp. small South African town

Droog-m'-keel. literally "dries-my-throat"; a shrub whose berry has dehydrant properties

Duiker; Duikerbok. antelope

Euphorbia. a tree exuding a milk-like toxic juice

Haikona. no (Xhosa)

Hamerkop. literally "hammerhead," a strange South African bird with a hammerlike projection of feathers on its head

Hardegat. difficult, intransigent

Here. Lord, in the Biblical sense

Hoopoe. colorful insectivorous bird

Kaffirmeid; meid. nigger-girl, girl, usually derogatory

Kloof. glen, ravine

Koppie. rock outcrop

Kranz. cliff

Lammervanger. a big South African eagle; literally, "lamb-catcher"

Mealies. maize

Middelmannetjie. crown of the road: the raised mound between the wheel tracks of a dirt road

Obbrigado. thank you (Portuguese)

Oom. uncle

Outspan. unharnessing ground for draft animals; also, the act of unharnessing animals

Poort. mountain pass

Regmaaker. first drink on the morning after; a "hair of the dog"

Riet. light cane

Rooikat. redcat; South African lynx

Samp. mealie mush

Slim. clever, shrewd

Sloot. dry gully

Spekboom. indigenous South African tree, small, with small round fleshy leaves

Spreeuw. a bird the size of a starling

Steenbras. thick-lipped sporting fish
Stompie. cigarette butt
Velskoens. hide shoes (lit: "skin-shoes")
Verneuk. cheat
Versigtig. careful
Verskriklik jags. over-amorous; usually applied to a woman
Vink. small yellow weaver bird